She felt a frisson of fear at the way Antonio had summoned thoughts and desires she had never experienced before.

Her marriage, and her position as Contessa Alfere-Tiziano, had taught Rissa the importance of putting on a good show for others. She had always been careful to do the right thing, and had never given in to temptation or emotion of any sort in public.

Frailty is for little people, Luigi had said.

Rissa certainly felt frail now, and guilty. Wicked thoughts crowded in upon her which she could not understand.

This dark stranger was forbidden and forbidding at the same time. It was a frightening *but exciting* combination.

GW00691715

Christina Hollis was born in Somerset, and now lives in the idyllic Wye valley. She was born reading, and her childhood dream was to become a writer. This was realised when she became a successful journalist, and lecturer in organic horticulture. Then she gave it all up to become a full-time mother of two, and run half an acre of productive country garden. Writing Mills & Boon® romances is another ambition realised. It fills most of her time, between complicated rural school runs. The rest of her life is divided between garden and kitchen, either growing fruit and vegetables or cooking with them. Her daughter's cat always closely supervises everything she does around the home, from typing to picking strawberries!

This is Christina's first book!

THE ITALIAN BILLIONAIRE'S VIRGIN

BY
CHRISTINA HOLLIS

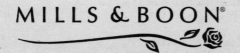

MILLS & BOON®

All the characters in this book have no existence outside the imagination of the author, and have no relation whatsoever to anyone bearing the same name or names. They are not even distantly inspired by any individual known or unknown to the author, and all the incidents are pure invention.

First published in Great Britain 2006
Paperback Edition 2007
Harlequin Mills & Boon Limited,
Eton House, 18-24 Paradise Road, Richmond, Surrey TW9 1SR

© Christina Hollis 2006

ISBN-13: 978 0 263 85291 2
ISBN-10: 0 263 85291 1

Set in Times Roman 10½ on 13 pt
01-0107-51902

Printed and bound in Spain
by Litografia Rosés, S.A., Barcelona

To my darling Martyn—
a perfect gentleman, who makes dreams come true.

CHAPTER ONE

BALMY afternoons in Tuscany were made for people-watching, although Rissa tried to hide her curiosity as Signor Mazzini guided her through the crowds.

'I am sure the late Count will have introduced you to the joys of the *passeggiata*, Contessa. It is that time when we all like to take the air.' Pink and perspiring, Mazzini threaded his client through the press of people strolling around the village square.

'My husband never brought me to Italy, *signor*. After our marriage, we rarely left America.' Rissa tried to keep the disappointment out of her voice. She had a lot of catching up to do. When Luigi had been alive, there had only been one, unhappy visit to her home in England. Now she was a free agent, her husband's debts were keeping her just as much a prisoner. Luigi's extravagant lifestyle had drained the Tiziano fortune of everything but the long-abandoned *palazzo* that bore his family's name. Rissa had only seen the place from a distance so far. Today was her first opportunity to enter the estate and look around the sole remaining Alfere-Tiziano property.

Trying to avoid actually being touched by Signor Mazzini's guiding hand, she walked across to the tall gates that protected the Tiziano estate. As Mazzini fumbled for his keys, Rissa got the strangest feeling that she was being watched. She had expected the villagers to be curious about her, but this felt somehow different.

She turned with a ready smile, but it faded instantly. A man was watching her from one of the many café tables set up around the village square.

'Buongiorno?'

She had felt bound to say something, but her observer stayed silent. He was only a few yards away, and could easily have replied, but he did not. He was well dressed, and might have been called handsome if not for his expression. He was piercing Rissa with a challenging glare. She caught her breath. No wonder she had sensed someone was looking at her. The intensity of that stare was enough to put anyone on their guard.

With a shiver, she followed Signor Mazzini into the safety of the estate. She was glad when he locked the gates behind him, but her relief was short-lived. Looking around the rampant wilderness, she saw that fallen trees had brought down the surrounding wall in several places. Her heart sank. Big repairs would mean big bills.

She had been blinded with love when she married Luigi. That love had changed over the years, as they'd come to terms with their secret sadness. Then his dazzling personality, which had kept her trapped like a rabbit in headlights, had been extinguished when his sports car went off the road at one hundred and twenty miles an hour.

Luigi's death had shocked Rissa out of her trance-like existence. Her next trauma had come when she'd discovered there was virtually no money left in any of Luigi's accounts, and that she was the last person in the world to bear the name of Alfere-Tiziano. That had given her a strong feeling of responsibility.

She *had* to keep up appearances, for Luigi's sake, and she *had* to see this mysterious *palazzo*. She had spent almost all her ready cash on a one-way ticket to Italy, and fallen instantly in love with the romance of the place. But she knew that this rundown estate could never pass to a rightful heir.

For a few weeks after Luigi's death, the heartbreak of their childless marriage had all but overwhelmed her again. Despite Rissa's shaky finances, when the office of AMI Holdings—apparently a great international construction company—had made her an exceptionally generous offer for the *Palazzo* Tiziano, she refused it point-blank. The sale would have given her more than enough money to move back home to London, but she felt she still had a duty to her adopted family name.

Her cash was now running dangerously low. Rissa had been almost tempted to reveal her problems and ask Signor Mazzini to contact AMI Holdings again, but two things stopped her. Luigi had been a proud man, and his heritage was at stake. She could not bear to think of his ancient family home being pulled down to make way for luxury holiday flats, which seemed to be the fate of every other historic house. There was another reason, too. A house in her name would give Rissa some security.

She knew that living in rented accommodation had been a terrible worry for the elderly couple that had brought her up. The only things Rissa possessed now were their love, and this place in the middle of nowhere. If somehow she could hang on to the house, and eventually earn enough to bring her adoptive parents out to live with her, she would do it.

Rissa had decided to give herself one year. If she had not succeeded by then, she would sell the *palazzo* and try to buy somewhere in England to share with her Aunt Jane and Uncle George, as she called her adoptive parents.

This romantic wreck of a house and its fairytale setting in the rolling Tuscan hills was her big chance to make a success of something. It was lovely, and there could be no question of selling. She *had* to improve on the hand fate had dealt her, so that she could bring her adoptive parents out to live here and bury her own demons of the past. Giving up was not an option.

It was a problem worthy of Sherlock Holmes, and Antonio Michaeli-Isola was not a man who liked puzzles. Brooding over his untouched *caffè freddo*, he observed the mating rituals of Italian youngsters. It was deceptively easy for them. The girls and boys eyed each other up in the hormone-drenched heat. Lack of money was the only obstacle to their happily-ever-after. Antonio had the opposite problem. He had all the women and all the money anyone could ever want— but he needed something else.

That 'something else' was the *Palazzo* Tiziano. He looked across the crowded village square to where high stone walls concealed his ultimate prize. He was not to be denied, and only one thing stood between him and his ideal home. The Contessa Alfere-Tiziano.

Without even meeting her, Antonio knew her type exactly. Women who had clawed their way into society were all the same. They were idle, amoral clotheshorses, who did nothing but tumble their male staff and bully their maids. Sex and money were the driving forces behind them. With Luigi Alfere-Tiziano dead, and the *palazzo* reputed to be a ruin, Antonio had expected 'her ladyship' to convert the dump into cash and disappear to the Hamptons as fast as her Manolo Blahnik heels could carry her. Instead, she was apparently determined the keep the old place.

It was inexplicable. In Antonio's experience, women simply did not behave like that. Getting the *palazzo* was obviously going to cost him more than money.

He watched a well-dressed man escort a girl across the street towards the *palazzo* gates. He tensed. Then his spirits soared. It must be the Contessa, being let into the estate by one of her staff. Antonio had expected a hard-faced Manhattan harridan. Instead, a slender, pretty girl glanced around nervously as she was led into the overgrown gardens beyond the estate walls.

Things are looking up, Antonio thought.

Getting his hands on the treasure of the Tizianos might be both easier and more enjoyable than he had expected.

A copy of the *Financial Times* was waiting for Antonio when he got back to the Excelsior hotel in Florence. Before checking the mail on his laptop, he flicked through the newspaper, and stopped when he saw his name in centimetre-high type.

Billionaire to fund new hospital, he read, grim-faced at the inaccuracies that underestimated his generosity and overstated his age. Antonio was not a vain man, so there was no question of demanding a retraction, but it showed how the media's Chinese whispers could distort facts. He read again the same old story, which they delighted in repeating. His mother was the daughter of a refugee. In acknowledgement of that family history, Antonio Michaeli-Isola still used part of her maiden name alongside that of his father, who had been a fisherman in Naples.

Unlike the glossy magazines, the *FT* did not linger over descriptions of Antonio's good looks and brooding Italian heritage. Unfortunately, like all other publications, it was still obsessed by the size of his bank balance. Antonio hated that.

Growing up in the shadow of poverty had taught him the need for hard work and self-reliance. Now he enjoyed putting something back into the community, but other people's fixation with the way he spent his money never failed to amaze him.

His expression flashed a warning. His features demanded respect rather than admiration. Growing up in the streets of Naples had left its mark on him. The dark eyes reacted with anger more often than merriment, and were rarely touched with a smile even when he appeared to be amused. He had learned as a child that the only person he could truly rely on was Antonio Michaeli-Isola. *If a job is worth doing, do it yourself* had been the maxim which had catapulted him from a two-roomed flat to corporate superstardom.

Now, men fawned over him when they were introduced. Women could not wait to paw him, and attached themselves to his arm like unlucky charms. Antonio had grown up on the wrong side of the tracks, where prostitution was often the only way some women could feed their children. He was not squeamish about the seamier side of life, but when wealthy women offered themselves to him like whores he found it difficult to disguise his disgust. His natural good manners were often tested to the limit.

He picked up the other newspaper the hotel had delivered and glanced through it, looking for the business section. Then a face on the society page caught his eye. It was she. The woman who had twice refused his company's offers for the *Palazzo* Tiziano. Antonio's expression hardened. Normally he never bothered to read the gossip columns. He knew everyone who was anyone in business, and preferred truth to speculation, but today he absorbed every word with relish.

From Riches—to Designer Rags? ran the headline.

Is the Contessa Alfere-Tiziano frittering away her late husband's millions?

Larissa Alfere-Tiziano has been selling off her inheritance at a rate of knots. Widowed by Count Luigi's love of fast cars, tragic Rissa has been getting ready for a little retail therapy by turning her late, lamented husband's property into hard cash.

The article included a photograph of the fawn-like beauty Antonio had watched walking into the estate that should, by rights, be his.

Antonio did not show emotion easily, but his brow lowered with every line. Appearances could certainly be deceptive. The girl he had seen following her flunkey into the *palazzo*'s grounds had looked as mild as milk. Antonio had foreseen no problem in sweet-talking her out of the house in a face-to-face meeting. Now he learned she was as shallow and greedy as all the rest of her sex.

With a thoughtful expression he folded the newspaper carefully and laid it down. Antonio might be rich, but he was not stupid. Two generous cash offers for the property had failed. Pushing more money at her would simply make the girl suspicious, and all the more likely to sit tight, hoping to push the stakes to ever more ridiculous heights. No, Antonio would have to employ guile. He would get his own way by more subtle means. Sex would feature, of course—he would never pass up such a delicious opportunity—but he would use it as bait to discover why she had sold off luxurious and better-placed properties for the greater glory of her bank balance, but not this one. Once he knew her motives, he could calculate the best way to move in for the kill.

Antonio leaned back in his chair and allowed himself a wolfish smile.

'I am delighted to make your acquaintance, Contessa.' The elderly woman made a creaking curtsy.

'Oh, please don't do that—Livia, isn't it?' Rissa shot a quick look at her land agent, Signor Mazzini. He nodded.

'Livia has looked after this place for as long as anyone can remember.'

Mazzini tried to oil his way past the housekeeper. He was eager to start a tour of the *palazzo*, but Rissa was more interested in the old lady.

'Thank you, Livia. The Alfere-Tiziano family must have been very grateful.'

'Ha!' The walnut-faced housekeeper muttered something else under her breath.

Despite her imperfect grasp of Italian, Rissa gathered that Luigi's aristocratic mother had been as generous towards Livia as she had been to Rissa. Both were commoners. As such they had been beneath the old Contessa's contempt, even though Rissa had married the last of the Alfere-Tiziano line.

Rissa did not know what to say in the face of Livia's discontent, but Mazzini came to her rescue.

'Come, Contessa, before the light fades. You will want to see around your new home.'

With a smile for Livia, Rissa allowed herself to be ushered from the draughty entrance hall into a warm, bright kitchen. One side of the room was almost filled by a huge, old-fashioned range. Reflections of its open fire danced across the gleaming copper pots and pans which hung over an enormous kitchen table. Seeing a plate set with chunks of ciabatta and a cone of goats' cheese, Rissa instantly turned to find the housekeeper. She did not have to look far. Livia was glowering at them from the threshold.

'I am sorry to have interrupted your meal, Livia. Come back to the table—Signor Mazzini and I can go somewhere else first.'

'No. This is meant for you, Contessa. It is your supper,' Livia announced with a look of triumph.

Rissa swallowed hard, wishing she had not been too proud to accept Mazzini's offer of a meal at the village trattoria.

'That's lovely, Livia. Shall I eat it now, or should we continue the tour, *signor*?' She looked to Mazzini for help, but Livia was quicker.

'You should eat now, so that I can wash up and still get home to the village before dark.'

Pulling a pitcher of milk from a bucket of cold water in the corner, Livia slopped some into a chipped mug and banged it down beside the makeshift meal. There were sour flakes floating on the watery white surface. Rissa looked back through the doorway into the hall, at the nearest portrait of one of the nobles who had lived in this house before her. There were huge pictures of them hanging all around the vestibule, each with raven-dark eyes and a piercing, humourless expression. *If this sort of food was good enough for them, then it will have to be good enough for me,* she thought, with more certainty than she felt.

Sitting down at the table, Rissa worked her way steadily through everything. She was determined not to turn up her nose at the stale bread or the sour milk, and managed it all.

'Thank you, Livia,' she said eventually, handing the housekeeper her empty plate and cup. Luckily her mobile rang before she had to add the words *That was lovely*.

'Auntie!' All the strain of the past weeks fell away and Rissa laughed with genuine pleasure. 'I was going to ring you as soon as I had a moment to myself—yes, I'm finally moving into Tiziano today. And as soon as I've sorted out a good room for you and Uncle, you can come here!'

Mazzini grimaced, and Rissa had the awful feeling she had said the wrong thing. Covering the mobile's mouthpiece, she questioned him with her eyes.

'A surveyor needs to check the upper floors before they can be trusted, and only two rooms on the ground floor are currently in use—this kitchen is one of them,' he hissed. Rissa's spirits sank.

'I hope you like camping.' She spoke to her aunt again. 'Apparently the house is all to pieces, but Signor Mazzini tells me it stands in ten hectares—'

'—of scrub and desolation.' Mazzini shook his head dolefully.

'So things can only get better!' Rissa reassured her aunt, with an attempt at cheerfulness. 'The couple who brought me up haven't had a night away from home in ten years,' she explained to Signor Mazzini when the call was over. 'They helped me through college, and they mean the world to me. I can't wait to see them again. It's been too long,' she said sadly.

'You have an *education*, Contessa?' said Mazzini, and Livia stared at her.

'Oh, yes—I studied Marketing and Media Studies. After graduating, some friends and I decided to spend a few months travelling before starting our careers. It didn't last long. I wanted to work my passage, sending money home when I could. I couldn't afford much socialising, so the other girls drifted off to LA and Las Vegas in search of more exciting company. Then one day Count Alfere-Tiziano's car got a flat tyre while he was burning up Route 66. He was marooned in the diner where I happened to be working. The rest, as they say, is history!'

Mazzini and Livia watched her warily. Not for the first time Rissa realised she had gone too far. Luigi had always scolded her for being too friendly with the staff. She shrank at the thought of what he would have said about her cheerful chatter. Then she decided that what Luigi would never know could not upset him. She straightened up, cleared her throat, and looked them both straight in the eyes.

'But that's all behind me now. I only have Aunt Jane and Uncle George to worry about. And the *Palazzo* Tiziano,' she added with a slight frown. 'You had better start my guided tour, Signor Mazzini. My world has been shrinking rapidly for the past few weeks, so I shall have to get used to it!'

Three hours later, Rissa was alone. Mazzini had swept off to Florence in his Alfa Romeo, while Livia had limped back down to the village. Thunder was growling around in the distance, and Rissa did not fancy sitting alone in the kitchen. She retreated to the tiny room that had been prepared for her. It must once have been a pantry, she decided, for the small, high window was barred and there was an underlying chill about the place. This was not helped by the inch-wide gap at the bottom of a door that led straight out into the garden.

In one corner of the room an ancient electric fire glowed. It added a bit of warmth, and Rissa sank down into a bed that was cosy, with soft blankets and sheets scented with lavender.

It was a pleasure to be hugged by a proper bed, with real linen and clouds of pillows, rather than struggling with ergonomically designed neck supports and a synthetic crackly duvet.

The only problem Rissa had was that her enjoyment could not be dimmed by sleep. She lay awake for hours, alert to every new sound. The ancient mansion creaked on its foundations as it settled for the night. From the kitchen next door she could hear noisy nibbling. Rissa did not know if it was a mouse…or something bigger. She did not feel like investigating. She could only lie in the darkness and wonder if it was a single creature, or whether it had company.

When the hands of her alarm clock crawled around for another hour and she still could not sleep, Rissa gave up. Getting out of bed, she switched on the light. Walking as noisily as she could over to where her suitcase rested across the arms of a squashy old armchair, she hoped that any four-legged residents of the house would be scared away before she could catch sight of them.

Among her favourite possessions was a small radio. She carried it with her everywhere. If she could tune into the World Service it would at least fill the lonely hours until dawn. Things never felt so bad in daylight—although how she would feel after a whole night without sleep, Rissa didn't like to think.

She had retrieved her transistor and was about to switch it on when she heard a plaintive cry from outside. The wind was getting up. Sounds of a gate on rusty hinges and a shutter swinging somewhere in the breeze made her more apprehensive than ever, but she was sure a cat was mewing out in the darkness. It was not a sound Rissa could ignore. She froze. The poor animal sounded like she felt—lonely and unsure. She waited. The sound grew closer, and more wavering.

There was nothing for it. Cautiously, Rissa went over and opened the door. The shaft of light she released lit undergrowth that crept up on the house from all sides. It also showed a big ginger cat, only feet away from where Rissa stood on the threshold. The creature had one front paw raised, and was jiggling its head to look past her, eyeing up the room beyond.

'Puss, puss, puss?' Rissa called. The wind whipped her words away like autumn leaves.

Greatly daring, Rissa took a few steps out into the night. The cat shrank into a half-crouch as she approached. As Rissa drew nearer, she could see that blood was staining the white toes of the cat's up-raised paw.

'You poor thing—let me see.' She reached out, but the cat sprang away. Even on three legs it was faster than Rissa could hope to be, but she followed it out into the darkness just beyond her lighted doorway. It was a mistake. Brambles tangling over the steep bank beyond the house snatched at her arms and legs. She tried to stop and go back, but the gradient and gravity swept her feet out from under her and she crashed into darkness.

Bruised, battered and out of breath, Rissa tried to drag herself upright, but gasped as a stab of pain shot through her ankle. A flash of lightning threw the undergrowth into sharp relief for a moment, before darkness returned, blacker than before. A spatter of icy rain scrabbled through the leaves. Now she was in the same position as the cat—or rather, worse. Rissa had no idea where she was. At least the cat must be local.

She sat down on the hard ground. The scent of pine resin and peppermint rose up from all around, and helped clear her head. She had to get back to the house. The door had been left standing wide open! Rissa could not bear to think what might be happening up there, but she tried to be optimistic. Perhaps the cat would go in and sort out the mouse in the kitchen? Based on her experiences so far, Rissa was not too hopeful *that* would happen.

A less-than-delicious supper, a depressing tour of the *palazzo* and now this tumble should have been enough to put her off the place for life. Instead, it sparked a new determination in her. Hauling herself upright, she managed to scramble painfully up the bank. It was a long way, etched with prickles and splinters. Rissa kept her head down and concentrated on where to put her feet, but she needed a boost to get her up the last little climb to the top. When she lifted her head, reassurance was the last thing she got.

Towering above her, silhouetted by the light from the open *palazzo* doorway, was the tall, muscular figure of a man.

CHAPTER TWO

'This is a dangerous place, Contessa.'

Rissa shrank back as he crouched down beside her. He was so near to her she could feel the warmth of him.

Thunder rolled a warning around the hills. She wondered whether she had more to fear from this stranger than she did from the weather and her new home combined.

'How do you know who I am?'

'This is a small village.' His voice was low but melodious. 'Everyone saw you arrive. They are hoping that by moving into the *palazzo* you will bring work to the village, but I know differently. There is not much hope of that, is there?' Seen in a flash of lightning, his face was hard and grim.

Rissa recognised him instantly. 'You were there—in the village square this afternoon. You were seated apart from the others, looking at me—'

Lightning crackled from the clouds again, giving Rissa a glimpse of his even white teeth. They were bared in a smile.

'That is so. I have returned here after…a long absence.'

'But what are you doing in my garden?'

Rissa might have been surprised by the sharpness of her tone if she had not been frightened half to death.

He put his head on one side, that interrogative stare pinning her down again. 'I wanted to have a look around, to see if the old place is still as my grandmother used to describe it to me.'

He continued to bend over her. Rissa reasoned that if he had been going to attack her he would have done so by now. She decided to try and stand up, then make a dash for the house.

'You aren't going to see much in the dark, *signor*,' she began, getting to her feet. But as she took a step she gasped.

He grabbed her as she crumpled, and stopped her from falling.

'Do you mind? Let go of me!' Rissa tried to shake off his hands, but he had a firm grip. The thunderstorm released a sudden spatter of huge raindrops in shining sheets, adding more urgency to her predicament.

'No—if you have an injury, Contessa, you may aggravate it further by trying to walk on it. Let's get you into the house.' Without waiting for her to agree, Antonio swept her up in his arms and began striding towards the lighted doorway.

'No—wait! There's a cat out here—it's injured—we can't leave it!' Rissa squirmed urgently in his grasp, made more desperate by the increasing deluge. It had soaked them both to the skin within seconds. He took no notice of her and strode on, an irresistible force. It was hopeless to try and fight. Shouting against the noise of the storm would be futile, too, and when they reached the sanctuary of the house he got in first.

'I shall go out and look for the animal as soon as you are—' He stopped. Then he laughed, water coursing from his rain-darkened hair across the subtle gold of his skin.

Rissa tore her gaze from her rescuer for long enough to see that the ginger cat was stretched out on a rug before the electric fire. It had beaten them back to the house and was basking in warmth while it licked its injured paw clean.

'I don't think you need to worry about him, Contessa. On the other hand, I must check to see if your injuries should be giving cause for concern.'

He was holding her indecently close to his body. She could feel his heart beating through the thin transparency of their wet clothes. It aroused a strange feeling within her. Hiding her uncertainty beneath a brisk tone, she spoke without taking her eyes off the cat.

'As you can see, this is my temporary bedroom, *signor*. Take me straight through that far door and into the kitchen, please.'

It had been a long time since she had been in the arms of a gorgeous man, and even longer since it had taken place in a bedroom.

'Very well,' her rescuer said sharply. 'And as you give orders as if I am your servant, Contessa, I should introduce myself. I am Antonio Isola.'

Closing the outside door, he crossed Rissa's room in a few easy strides and entered the kitchen. For an instant the storm threw enough light through the windows to let him place her down safely on a chair. Then he found a switch and flooded the room with harsh electric light.

Rissa blinked. The tall man standing in her doorway was shrink-wrapped by his sodden shirt and jeans. His clothes clung to every contour, leaving nothing to the imagination. Biceps and pectorals thrust against thin cotton made almost invisible by the rain. With a gasp, Rissa saw a full pelt of dark body hair casting a shadow beneath his white top. The spell was only broken when she realised that his slow, spreading smile meant that the hard beads of her nipples must be equally visible through her negligee. She threw one arm protectively across her chest.

'Could you fetch me my robe please, *Antonio*? It's draped over the bedhead.' Rissa waved her other hand dismissively towards her bedroom.

'Is the cat all right?' she said, when he returned with the less-than-practical dressing gown Luigi had bought her for their honeymoon. That time in her life had been such a whirlwind of high hopes, dreams and expectations. If only they had been fulfilled. Luigi would have left the *palazzo* with a legitimate heir and not just *me*, Rissa thought sadly.

'The cat has settled himself down to keep watch on a mouse hole. I think we can assume he will be OK, Contessa.'

He spoke in heavily accented English, a musical sound that did nothing to settle Rissa in her chair. She looked away quickly. Focussing on her ankle, she probed it gingerly.

Antonio advanced and crouched in front of her. 'Try wiggling your toes.'

Rissa did as she was told. Slipping his hand around her ankle, Antonio cradled her heel. Gently but firmly he used the fingers of his other hand to test for movement. The pain had almost disappeared, but Rissa still flinched.

'There is nothing broken, but you will have some magnificent bruises, Contessa.' He surveyed her with practised eyes.

Before Rissa could complain, they both stiffened at a sound from outside.

Antonio vanished towards the door, and a minute later Rissa heard Livia's voice, raised in agitation. Trying out her left foot with care, Rissa made her way over to her bedroom.

The housekeeper had the ginger cat gripped in her arms and was scolding him and crooning by turns. She was speaking so quickly that Rissa's Italian could barely keep up. Antonio obliged with a translation.

'Fabio escaped from Livia's new lodgings at her sister's house in the village, tearing a claw in the process. He made straight for his old haunts. Livia has been frantic, so she arrived for work early in the hope she would find him here.'

Rissa looked at her travel clock in amazement. 'It's five o'clock already and I haven't slept a wink!'

'A beautiful *contessa* like you will not have to worry about that,' Antonio said silkily, with a smile that did not reach his eyes. 'Rich women are well known for their ability to spend whole days languishing in bed, are they not?'

'Not *this* one,' Rissa said firmly. She was careful not to mention that Livia probably had more disposable income than she did. 'I've got a busy day ahead. I need to sort myself out a new room, because it sounds like Livia has given me hers and I cannot allow that. You must come back here to live, Livia. This is your home.'

The housekeeper beamed, squeezing Fabio around the midriff until the cat's eyes bulged.

'In the meantime, would you mind providing Antonio with some breakfast, please?' Rissa went on. 'He was kind enough to help me. The least we can do is to offer him some hospitality.'

'I don't know, Contessa.' The housekeeper stuck out her lower lip and looked Antonio up and down suspiciously.

Rissa was not entirely taken in by Antonio's charm either, but she had to repay him in some way. A stand had to be made.

'He will be happy with whatever you were going to make for me, I am sure.'

'He is a stranger, Contessa,' Livia grumbled, still eyeing Antonio.

'And so am I,' Rissa said firmly. 'Now, if you would both

excuse me, I must get ready for the day and find myself a new room.'

There were warm towels in a cupboard beside the range. Rissa took out an extra one and handed it to Antonio. He looked momentarily surprised before resuming his air of amused indifference.

By the time Rissa returned to the kitchen, showered, and dressed in a short-sleeved shirt and jeans, breakfast was ready. Breads and cold meats were laid out on the table, together with glasses of fresh orange juice. It looked far better than the miserable meal that had greeted her the day before.

Rissa stopped and stared—but not at the breakfast. It was the shock of seeing Livia smile. It was the first time since Rissa's arrival that she had seen the housekeeper grin at her. Then she saw what was amusing the old woman. Antonio had stripped off completely and was standing beside the range, pouring out espresso. A thick white towel was wrapped around his narrow waist. He looked amazing.

Giving both Antonio and Livia a casual greeting, Rissa sat down at the big old kitchen table. As she took a roll from the bread basket and began her breakfast, she saw that Antonio's skin was the same tone of clear light gold all over. It did not take much to visualise that glorious colour continuing beneath the tightly wrapped snowy towelling. Rissa found herself drawing in a long, appreciative breath. Reluctantly she realised that, despite all her enforced celibacy, female hormones were a law to themselves. Antonio was a perfect Alpha male, from the lean lines of his muscles to that mass of dark chest hair.

Rissa passed the tip of her tongue over her lips. Her breasts were tingling. Her nipples pressed against the lacy bra she was wearing beneath her tee shirt, and became painfully obvious. She felt heat rising to her cheeks. How could her body betray her like this when it had been so long since Luigi had shown any interest in her? She had thought all passionate feelings had died in the early days of her marriage. The memory of how Antonio had held her close when he carried her into the house must have triggered some sort of reaction. It had certainly alerted all her senses.

Antonio placed a small cup of dark coffee beside her, then offered one to Livia. The housekeeper looked aghast, and took a step back.

'You are *that* sort of employer, then, are you, Contessa?' Antonio announced, putting his own cup down on the table and taking a seat opposite Rissa. His eyes locked with hers. He seemed oblivious to the effect he was having on her. As a respectable widow, Rissa knew she should be glad he was so detached, but while her head told her one thing her body rebelled with feelings of its own.

'Livia is quite welcome to sit and have coffee while I discuss the day ahead with her,' Rissa said briskly.

'I'm glad you want to get down to business straight away. The quicker we get started, the quicker this place can be restored.'

Rissa looked at him blankly. *'We?'*

Antonio concentrated on cutting himself a square of focaccia. He had to hide a cynical smile. If everything went according to his plan, the *Palazzo* Tiziano would soon be returning to its rightful owner, not just its former glory. Naturally he would not be telling the Contessa that. He intended that she would be far, far away by the time he took possession.

'You speak reasonable Italian, Contessa.'

'Thank you—'

'But that is not enough to deal with tradesmen and artisans. Livia tells me the house and grounds need a great deal of repair—indeed, I must come with you to choose your new room to make sure it is structurally sound. It is lucky we met when we did. You have great need of someone who is experienced. In property development,' he added, after a significant pause.

'Do you have anyone in mind, Antonio?'

She wanted him to persuade her, he thought caustically. The wiles of women always annoyed him.

'I am fully qualified in every department.'

Rissa did not doubt it.

'That is, I could become your project manager, Contessa. You need someone to tell you what work must be done, in what order, and who can be relied upon to get those things achieved quickly and efficiently. My first task will be to conduct a detailed survey of this house from top to bottom.'

'Wait a minute, Antonio! How do I *know* that you are the right man for the job? And can I afford you?'

'The Palazzo Tiziano cannot afford to lose me.' Antonio took a leisurely sip of coffee. 'This house needs me… you need me,' he added, but at his own, slightly suggestive pace.

'I shall have to ring Signor Mazzini.' Rissa was uneasy. She didn't know if she should tell him quite everything about this Antonio. Although he sounded the part, and the place definitely needed a good manager, she didn't quite trust him.

However, the sooner she could get the house into a fit state for her aunt and uncle to move in, the happier Rissa would be. Her adoptive family had taken her in as a baby, but their desperate desire to give her the best of everything had meant they had little left for themselves. As soon as she'd grown old enough to appreciate the sacrifices they had made for her, Rissa had been determined to pay them back. She had taken her first Saturday job at fourteen, waiting at tables. When she had been offered a university place it had been natural for her to contribute to the expenses. She had sent as much money home as possible—until the day when...

As well as being a fairytale romance, it had seemed such a wonderful opportunity at the time. Luigi Alfere-Tiziano had walked into the diner where she'd worked and it had been love at first sight—at least as far as Rissa had been concerned. In Luigi's case it had been more a cocktail of lust and rebellion against his mother. The love had come later.

A whirlwind courtship of champagne, gifts and starry nights had made Rissa feel like a princess. She had been Cinderella in the arms of her very own Prince Charming. Only when Luigi had taken her home to show off her multi-carat engagement ring had Rissa realised she'd fallen into a trap.

Antonio watched her as carefully as Fabio the cat had been watching that mouse hole. She was miles away, he thought, noticing emotion drawing down over her eyes like a veil until she blinked it away.

'I am the perfect man for your job,' he announced brusquely.

Shaking off her memories, Rissa came down to hard, un-promising earth.

'So you say, Antonio. But how do I *know* that? Magazines like *Harpers & Queen* and *Country Life* have beautiful build-ings like the Palazzo Tiziano in them all the time. It will take expertise, time and a great deal of money to return my house and estate to the condition they should be in. How do I know that you have the knowledge and expertise it needs?' She was frowning. After settling with Luigi's creditors, Rissa now had to watch every penny—but there was no way she was going to tell Antonio that.

'You also mentioned time, Contessa. You and I both have plenty of that.' Antonio flexed his powerful shoulders. 'Hard work never killed anyone. You can plan the restoration and detailed budgets—under my guidance, of course. I will organise the workforce, and together we shall work to make the Palazzo Tiziano the beautiful place it should be. Of that I am certain,' he decided. 'To convince you to agree, I shall work for nothing.'

He smiled to himself. 'Billionaire for hire' had a good ring to it—but what the hell? He didn't need the money, and it would be sheer pleasure to help put this house back into shape, knowing it would soon be his. He would work on her from the inside, he thought, with considerable satisfaction.

Finishing his breakfast, he pushed away his plate and stood up. Rissa had been silenced by his generous offer, but now she had to stifle a gasp. He loomed over her in a way that brought warmth powering through her veins again. With an effort she collected her thoughts, then wished she hadn't. They involved the sensation of his hands grasping her again, perhaps even pulling her across the table for a passionate kiss.

She cleared her throat and looked up at him. It was a mistake. The intensity of his expression caught her heart and slammed it against her ribs. His lips were parting in a half-smile, a hint of white teeth gleaming against gold skin. It was an expression that said: *Come on, kiss me. You know you want to…*

Rissa's hazel eyes became dark pools of sensuality as she wondered what it would be like to have her own lips pressed against that firm mouth, to be silenced by—

'Contessa—' Antonio's voice cut through her feverish thoughts. With a shock, Rissa realised her breath was coming in little gasps, and she could only imagine the guilty depth of her blush.

'This will be a formal working arrangement, Contessa.'

'Of course!' Rissa jumped to her feet, shocked to discover the effect he was having on her body. She felt as frail as a kitten, and had to grip the tabletop for support.

'I assume you have no objection to employing me on that understanding?'

'Of course not, Antonio. Although I will reimburse you as soon as the house is in a fit state to be mortgaged, so please keep a note of all the hours you work and any expenses you may incur.'

He had not expected that. Looking down at the good, yet understated watch on his wrist, he thought quickly.

'No. That will not be necessary. Work on the Palazzo Tiziano will stop me getting bored, and keep my skills current. And now—I think Livia's clothes-dryer should have finished with my things.'

'I'll fetch them,' Livia said quickly, heading out to the ramshackle laundry area.

'Good—that allows me the chance to give you some advice, Contessa.' His voice dropped to a whisper. Planting both hands firmly on the table, he leaned towards Rissa. As he did so, her eyes fixed on the discreet crucifix swinging gently from a fine silver chain around his neck.

'Yes?' Rissa managed to sound detached, but only because she was not looking directly at him.

'There is no need to undress a man with your eyes when he is wearing only a towel.'

'*What?*' Rissa squeaked. Livia returned at exactly the wrong moment, and exploded with laughter.

'I saw the way you were looking at me. Running that glance over every centimetre of my body.'

'Never!'

Although the kitchen table was between them, Rissa took a step back.

'All English women desire our men.' Livia chuckled unhelpfully. 'And Antonio is surely a prime specimen, *signora*!'

'You see?' Antonio arched one dark eyebrow. 'Livia acknowledges your feelings, even when you cannot. It is an accepted fact that those in power like to dabble with the lower orders. *Droit du seigneur*, I think it is called.' He shrugged. 'So, if during the long, cold nights here you need a few personal services to warm your heart, and perhaps a few other places—'

'No!' Rissa snapped, desperate to regain some sort of authority.

How on earth was she going to make her new home a fitting memorial to the great house of Alfere-Tiziano when her staff enjoyed so much fun at her expense?

Antonio had dressed and left an hour before, but Rissa still could not get him out of her mind. Any woman would have to be made of stone not to be moved by that body, and his charmingly dangerous attitude. She walked through the *palazzo*, trying to decide where she wanted Antonio to survey with a view to providing her with a proper room, but she could take nothing in. Restless and uncertain, she was troubled by the feverish ache running through her body. It would have been unusual enough if this handsome stranger had only tempted her. The real shock was the extent of her physical arousal. For years marriage had persuaded her that she was sadly lacking in that department.

Thoughts of Antonio super-heated her in a way her late husband had never warmed her. Rissa had been married for five difficult years, but Antonio had worked some sort of magic within seconds. She felt a frisson of fear at the way he had summoned thoughts and desires she had never experienced before. Her marriage, and her position as Contessa Alfere-Tiziano, had taught Rissa the importance of putting on a good show for others. She had always been careful to do the right thing, and had never given in to temptation or emotion of any sort in public.

Frailty is for little people, Luigi had said.

Rissa certainly felt frail now, and guilty. Wicked thoughts crowded in upon her which she could not understand. After all, she had never made a success of sex with Luigi, and Antonio had made no secret of his scorn for her title and position.

This dark stranger was forbidden and forbidding at the same time. It was a frightening combination—but exciting.

CHAPTER THREE

'AH...SO many beautiful clothes!' Livia murmured next morning as Rissa began to unpack.

They were standing in the rooms that Antonio, not Rissa, had chosen as her suite. He had probed the upstairs rooms in detail the day before, working with the air of an expert. Most of the first floor had been pronounced sound enough for immediate use. The remaining salons and the top storey would need work, but for the moment Rissa could breathe again. Perhaps the place wasn't in such a desperate state after all.

At the moment her new rooms were nothing more than large, dusty spaces with breathtaking views out over the surrounding hills. Looking straight down, the prospect was not so lovely. Rissa's overgrown estate would need a lot of work before she could bear to gaze on what should be palatial gardens. The wrought-iron balconies outside her windows were too delicate with age to walk on, but at least Antonio was more optimistic than Mazzini had been about the *palazzo*'s interior.

Rissa's self-appointed project manager had been going over the house with great care. In here, he had made a list of things to be done, but they were only cosmetic touches like decorating and minor repairs. That could wait. The main aim was to get the whole place as habitable as her new bedroom.

Not that it seemed very habitable to Rissa, as she gazed around at all the dust and cobwebs. Two huge oak cupboards took up most of one wall, flanking a marble fireplace. These would have taken all her belongings with room to spare, but when Livia had opened the cupboard doors stale, musty air had rushed out and put both women off the idea. Instead of storing everything in the cavernous interiors, Rissa and Livia had rigged up makeshift shelves from bricks and old floorboards. Clothes by Armani and Moschino now had to hang from the curtain rails. They did the job of curtains far better than the old moth-eaten drapes, and were much more colourful.

'There will not be room here for a fraction of your things, *signora*,' Livia said sourly. Antonio had persuaded the housekeeper to thaw a little, but when he left the room he always managed to take Livia's smile with him.

'That won't matter, Livia. I shall be selling most of it. There must be stores dealing in second-hand designer clothes in Florence.'

'There is a charity shop in the village…'

'Yes, I noticed it. Unfortunately I must be practical. There is far too much stuff here—you've said that yourself. I might as well sell some to help fund repairs to the *palazzo*. Any proceeds left over when this place is perfect and we open to the public can be pledged to the charity shop. How's that?'

'I do not know what your agent, Signor Mazzini, or for that matter Signor Antonio will say to such an idea.' Livia clicked her tongue. 'Foreigners! *Ha!* It was bad enough when the place was going to be knocked down and the estate filled with holiday homes. I suppose we should be grateful that you only wish to fill the gardens with elderly English ladies!'

Rissa was so horrified by Livia's earlier words that she let the slur on her own plans pass without comment.

'Somebody wanted to demolish the *palazzo*?' Astounded, she looked around at its shabby grandeur. 'But this house is so beautiful—and it must be full of history. What would have happened to all the family portraits downstairs?'

'No family—no portraits.' Livia shook her head heavily. 'Signor Mazzini was approached by an office in Cardiff— where they play the rugby. Although not as well as in Italy, of course,' she added with defiance.

Livia's hidden depth of sporting knowledge impressed Rissa, but she was more interested in what might have been going on behind her back.

'Signor Mazzini told you what has been going on?'

'Things become common knowledge in Monte Piccolo very quickly. Some billionaire property developer wanted to come here and change everything,' Livia's tone showed she had little time for the rich. 'Signor Mazzini did not want that. On the day of your husband's funeral he told the company you would never sell.'

Rissa was puzzled. 'But at that time I didn't know anything about the *palazzo*…'

'Signor Mazzini knew the village would not want change. He must have been answering in everyone's best interests, Contessa.'

'Yes…' Rissa frowned. 'And he was quite right. Everything must be done to secure the *palazzo*'s future as it stands, for the good of the village.'

The housekeeper looked at her sideways. 'But you are not a local, *signora*. Why should you care?'

'My husband's mother was a local, Livia. She was proud of their ancient name. A sense of history and continuity in a changing world makes us what we are. That is why I am determined to keep this house, no matter what.'

It was just as well Rissa truly believed in what she was saying. The scornful look on Livia's face could leave her in no doubt about the housekeeper's feelings on the matter.

With Livia's help, Rissa sorted her luggage into those items she would be keeping, the ones that could be given away to the charity shop, and designer pieces to be resold at a good price. Rissa had always been careful with her possessions, and her clothes were immaculate. The most expensive items were invariably those that had been worn only once, or sometimes not at all. Luigi had bought her many designer pieces, but his taste had been for the skimpy and revealing. He had not been a man to put up with any objections, so Rissa had persuaded him to invest in several silk jackets for her to wear over the strapless tops and cutaway evening gowns.

Pleased with the amount they had achieved, Rissa looked at her Rolex. It was not yet ten a.m. Her heart leapt as she realised there was time to go exploring in the grounds before the sun rose too high.

Antonio watched her hurry down the wide stone steps at the back of the *palazzo*, noting that her turned ankle looked as good as new. He had already been to see Mazzini, and knew which way the wind was blowing. The agent had been suspicious of Antonio's self-appointment as the Contessa's right-hand man, and the officious little man had insisted on ringing her to check. From the way he had spoken to the Contessa over the phone, Antonio guessed there was more to Mazzini's interest in the girl's welfare than mere business.

Antonio saw and heard everything, but said little. It suited him to keep Rissa guessing about his own domestic arrangements. He had a good car, and commuting from Florence would be no problem. Working on the *palazzo* would be a pleasure, not a grind, and he intended to arrive early and leave late each day. This would give him plenty of time for roaming the grounds unobserved.

He'd discovered that the Tiziano estate had plenty of possibilities. Close study of the place showed it to be a rare treasure. The girl must be aware of its value, too, or she would have sold it. Antonio knew that Mazzini was also keen to get his hands on the *palazzo*. If Rissa would not sell, then there was only one way either man could take legal possession of the estate. Antonio smiled. They must both be considering similar tactics. It was a method particularly enjoyed by Italians, although men the world over would kill for the chance to get lucky in property by seducing such a prize.

He laughed silently as he studied Rissa from his vantage point on top of the estate's crumbling bell tower. She would never think of looking up, so he was able to watch her picking her way gingerly through the scrub and tumbled stones. A perfect example of her type, he thought cynically. Who else would dress in close-fitting white jeans and a pale lemon tee shirt for a jungle expedition?

He wondered idly what it would be like to take her to bed. Over the years he had enjoyed women from every social strand, but they had all shared one desire—a wedding ring, marrying them to Antonio's fortune. Their problem was that

Antonio had no illusions about the venal, grasping ways of women. He had seen many other rich men fall under the spell of beautiful girls. The affairs always followed a predictable pattern. Once the ring was securely on a girl's finger, she would develop a serious addiction to spending. It might begin honestly enough, on designer labels or prestigious parties, but it was never long before the muscle-bound personal trainer moved in, and cocaine replaced the *petit fours*.

Antonio had managed to avoid the honey traps of these 'legal whores', as he called them. To turn the tables and pass himself off as nothing more than a builder, eager for a rich woman's favour, appealed to his sense of humour.

He would be enjoying the Contessa while planting worries in her mind about the *palazzo*. He had not been able to regain it by offering a good price, so he would have to use psychology. A young, attractive widow, alone in a foreign land, would be desperate for someone to lean on—especially when she heard of the Tiziano Curse. His smile widened. If she *were* superstitious, she would be out of the place like a shot. If not, she would still quiver and appeal to him with wide-eyed innocence. He could sense it. The way she had looked at his half-naked body told him everything.

His feral instinct had been to take her there and then, tumbling the neatly laid table in their shared urgency. If the housekeeper had not been there he probably would have done, he thought wolfishly. But then his smile faded. The only way to bring it back was to remember the way the girl's body had responded to him so seductively each time their paths crossed.

Dark sickles of swifts screamed over the derelict olive groves. They made Rissa look up sharply. She was wondering if the birds would disappear south for the winter, like English ones did, when a slight movement caught her eye. On top of the *campanile* a silhouette stood out against the hard blue sky. Rissa recognised it immediately.

'Antonio! What are you doing up there? It can't be safe!'

'It is safe enough, Contessa,' he called back. Dodging out of sight, he reappeared a few moments later at the open door of the old tower. 'Although I do not recommend that you enter until a few running repairs have been carried out.'

'Is that what you were doing—checking it out?' Approaching cautiously, she glanced up at the crumbling stonework, but Antonio's body kept attracting her gaze like a magnet. He was wearing a plain white tee shirt, which made the healthy colour of his skin glow even more desirably. His jeans were old, but well fitting, and speckled with paint of several different colours. Hands on hips, he watched her draw closer. It was a stance that made Rissa's mouth go dry.

'I went to see your man Mazzini earlier this morning, Contessa. You should be aware that he resents your presence here.'

'Rubbish! Why would he say such a thing?'

'Because he wants this house for himself?'

'He advised me not to accept the offer made by that AMI company, Antonio. If he had wanted to get rid of me, he would have made more fuss when I confirmed I wasn't going to sell to anyone.'

Antonio's dark eyes were watchful as he calculated what he should try next. He wanted to plant doubts in her mind, but there was a fine line between the scary and the unbelievable. After a pause, he clicked his fingers with apparent inspiration.

'He must have been thinking of that old Monte Piccolo saying, Contessa!'

'What old saying?'

'That the village will fall if the Tiziano estate goes out of the family.'

'That's ridiculous,' Rissa said, but something behind his laughter made her add, 'Isn't it? I expect it's a story made up to fool credulous locals—like the myth about the Tower of London needing its ravens if the English monarchy is to continue.'

'Ah, you have seen through us, Contessa.' Antonio's voice was low with amusement. 'Of course that is it! We locals were particularly lucky in the nineteen-forties, when a great earthquake happened at the precise moment the owners were removed from Tiziano. It was a complete coincidence, of course, but one which gave the old threat a whole new lease of life.'

His words brought Rissa up short. 'Earthquake? Do we get earthquakes here?'

'Yes, *we* do.' He emphasised her isolation heavily. 'Although they rarely happen. However, there was one time, when the eccentric bachelor Count Angelo had abandoned the place to go on a barefoot pilgrimage to Rome. The village was shaken to such an extent that every building except the church and *palazzo* was razed to the ground.'

Rissa gasped, but Antonio merely shrugged. 'Wooden houses are as easily destroyed as they are rebuilt. Nevertheless, leaving the *palazzo* without a Tiziano might not be worth the risk, if you believe in such things.'

'Oh, no!' Rissa's eyes widened in alarm as a terrible thought struck her. 'I'm only a Tiziano by marriage! Does that count?'

'Who knows?' Antonio grinned. 'In any case, that old wives' tale is probably no more true than the Tiziano Curse.'

This was too much. Rissa hoped he was making it up, but she had to know. She had been avoiding eye contact with him because of the effect it had on her, but she steeled herself to ignore his melting milk chocolate gaze and keep to the matter in hand. 'Signor Mazzini never mentioned any curse.' She managed to convey some suspicion.

Although he was unfazed, it was Antonio's turn to avoid meeting her worried gaze.

'He wouldn't. He wants you safely settled in here so that he can marry you and complete his master plan—a Tiziano in the *palazzo*, and him as master of the village. That is where this so-called curse is supposed to come into play. It is said that any faithless wife living here will attract the dogs of doom.'

Rissa did not know what to say. It sounded ridiculous. Antonio was looking as though he had no time for such old stories, but there was often some sort of historical basis for these things…

'I suppose you will feel happier among my *credulous* people if you have a man in charge, Contessa.' He threw more words at her like poison darts.

'Wait a minute.' Rissa narrowed her eyes. 'There's a great hall in there, lined with grim portraits of warriors and redoubtable women. They all managed to survive here. I've been looking at the dates. Most of them lived into old age— with the exception of some of the angry-looking young men,' she added thoughtfully.

It was Antonio's turn to frown, but before he could question her Rissa supplied an answer.

'All those other members of Luigi's family braved the curse, so I shall have to manage it, too. You've said you'll work here while the place is being restored, Antonio. If you're so worried about my welfare, why not live here, in the site office? There's plenty of room. You could be here 24/7.'

Antonio threw his hands up in despair. 'That is a horrible phrase! You would give a stranger like me such licence? Just because I have told you I am good at my job, Contessa? And you call *us* credulous.'

'I am beginning to hate that word.' Rissa pursed her lips. 'Of course I wouldn't act on anything you said without—'

'Stop.' He held up his hand, silencing her. 'I have already arranged everything with Signor Mazzini. All my professional qualifications are to be couriered to him, as necessary—although I think I impressed him sufficiently by force of personality alone. But you should not take everyone at face value, Contessa. Tell me, did Luigi Alfere ever let you out on your own?'

'No, as it happens.'

'The man must have had at least a grain of sense, then.'

Temporarily lost for words, Rissa stared down at her red sandals, which were covered in dust.

'Can we start work now?' She looked up at him apprehensively.

'When you are so clearly ready for business?' he mocked. 'For instance, where is your measuring tape, your notebook and pens?'

Rissa was ahead of him there. With a flourish she pulled all the necessary bits and pieces from her back pockets. Her cheeks were burning, but this time it was not only the effect of pulsing female hormones. How *dared* this man approve of the way Luigi had kept her a virtual prisoner? A cage was a cage, even when it was gilded with twenty-four-carat gold.

'I mean business, Antonio,' she said firmly. 'Perhaps we ought to get to work before the ancestors catch up with us.'

Turning on her heel, she stalked off. Antonio took a moment to admire her curvaceous walkaway. That was before she threw a mischievous look over her shoulder at him.

'Come on!'

Antonio knew then that he should have trusted his instincts at their first meeting. He ought to have thrown her onto that bed, accepting the invitation flaunted by the fullness of those beautiful breasts. Her dark, dilated pupils and parted lips told him she would not have resisted, even if his mouth had followed his fingertips in exploring and enjoying every centimetre of her.

He grimaced. She is no different from any other woman, he reminded himself, and I know what they are like.

If his real identity were revealed to her she would have only one reaction to that sort of treatment: gimme, gimme, gimme—money, trinkets, and expense accounts…it was the way of the world.

Antonio shook himself and strode after the Contessa, his mind almost on the job in hand. No woman was worth all this agonising. Property was the only thing that mattered. Land and his family's heritage must be his only interest.

It took the sight of Antonio plunging through a tangle of olives and vines to put his high-handed attitude out of Rissa's head. More than once she caught herself gasping as a vision danced in her mind of Antonio's thrusting arrogance being turned on her, of him taking her there on the dry dusty ground, or pressing her up against one of the ancient oak trees as his hands pushed aside her flimsy clothing and—

She put one hand to her brow, dizzy with an image of his sensual power and complete domination.

'The sun is too much for you, Contessa?'

'No—no, not at all, thank you, Antonio. I'm finding all the facts and figures you are firing at me a bit hard to visualise, that's all,' she improvised, fanning herself with her notebook.

'Come—sit over here in the shade while I check the condition of this terrace wall,' he ordered. His plan was beginning to work rather better than he had imagined. OK, so he couldn't seem to frighten the girl with folk tales, but something else was definitely happening. If he could convince her that restoring the *palazzo* would be a mammoth project after all, that might scare her away. She would be more interested in choosing colour schemes for the interior than in organising essentials such as ground works and utilities.

Relieved that Antonio seemed to be engrossed in his work, Rissa began concentrating on her own calculations. Luigi might not have wanted her to go on and take up a career in marketing, but she could still use the things she had learned on her course. She had been streets ahead of her contemporaries at university, but had always brushed aside their praise with embarrassment. In contrast, her talent for spotting opportunities could be given full expression here. The hardest part would be convincing Signor Mazzini and Antonio that her plans could work.

She moved restlessly. Even the thought of Antonio's name could have a startling effect. The slightest pressure of jeans and tee shirt on the curves of her body now made her feel entirely feminine. She felt as though she was powerless before the heat of his raw sensuality. It was madness. She no longer needed him to stand before her to obtain this effect—simply the sound of him crashing through the undergrowth like a wild animal sent pulses of desire through the most intimate parts of her body. She had never felt like this before—not even in the first heady days of Luigi's courtship.

When Antonio returned to her side, the taunting smile on his lips almost stopped her noticing that his tee shirt was damp from pushing through wet foliage. It was clinging closely to him, and once again it was almost, but not quite, transparent. It showed off every contour of his body, the white fabric emphasising the smooth firmness of his bare arms. Rissa felt her face growing hotter by the moment. She began searching for a clean page in her notebook. Flustered, she dropped it, and her pen—the Mont Blanc Luigi had given her on their first date—rolled away towards a crack in the old stonework.

Rissa dived for it at exactly the same moment Antonio darted forward. They collided as the pen disappeared into the crevice. Rissa clutched at Antonio for support, but the collision and the sudden nearness of him was too much. The air was forced from her lungs. As she gasped, she drew in all the fresh, warm fragrance of him. Skin against skin, she felt the firmness of his muscles gliding beneath her fingers. The texture of him made the fine cotton of his shirt feel coarse in comparison.

'Well, Contessa, that was close!' Low and confiding, his voice caressed the small space between them.

'What do you mean? I've lost my pen, and it was a present from my late husband—'

'I didn't mean that. I meant this.'

He looked down at her fingers, which had closed convulsively on his arm. Rissa let go, as though his body was as inflammable as hers.

'You don't need to restrain yourself with me, Contessa. Feel free to let yourself go.'

Rissa scrambled to her feet and backed away.

'I—I don't know what you mean...' she began, desperately trying to stop her mind dwelling on what it would be like to feel him returning her touch, to stop imagining his naked flesh pressed against hers in that dance as old as time—

'Oh, but I think you do.' In one smooth movement Antonio stripped off his damp tee shirt and tucked it into his belt. His eyes were laughing as he moved softly towards her. 'You have lost a treasured memento of your husband. After so recent a bereavement, no one could blame you for breaking down at such a loss.'

Antonio's *double entendre* had been deliberate—a test to see if she really was as bad as all the other women of her class. He watched her expression change, and his smile became one of triumph. He had proved to himself that she was no different from the working girls on the streets of his home town, trading their bodies for the fleeting advantage of money. At least Neapolitan whores were honest in their dealings. *This* girl had married a man who had given himself airs for nothing more than the meaningless advantage of a title. Surely, he thought, if she had loved Luigi Alfere in the way a wife should, there would have been tears, or at least some expression of grief. Instead, she looked embarrassed and ashamed.

Antonio's expression hardened. Instead of thinking about her late husband, she had been thinking about *him*. At the same time, Antonio had been imagining her willing body entwined with his as they tasted each other's arousal...

With a great effort of will he turned away from temptation and went to pull a metal bar from a long abandoned pile of scaffolding poles. Using it to prise apart the flagstones and retrieve her pen would distract him from the magnet of her body.

The problem was that this girl was altogether too desirable. Antonio planned to get her house. It was nothing more than another of his business ventures, he told himself, and no woman could be allowed to distract him from his goal. Desire was wayward, and he had no time for that—or a sitting tenant.

When Antonio had pulled her pen from its hiding place, Rissa accepted it graciously. Then she suggested they should go back to the kitchen and start on some paperwork. Livia had already told her she would be busy there all day. Rissa could not think of a better passion-killer than the respectable Italian matron bustling about while she and Antonio worked on plans—and she certainly needed a passion-killer.

Rissa had hoped her nights at the *palazzo* would be better now that she had a proper room. It was not to be. That night she spent restless hours going over what Antonio had told her about the Curse of Tiziano. At least she was no longer alone in the house. Livia and Fabio the cat had moved back into their lair next to the kitchen. At first the old lady had been aghast at the thought of Rissa sleeping in one of the abandoned rooms. Then the deliveries had begun. First Antonio had hired men from the village to lug a comfortable new bed up to Rissa's suite. Then a convoy carrying the rented site office had arrived, bringing with it portable heaters and dehumidifiers. Satisfied that the Contessa would be catered for, whatever the weather might throw at them, Livia had agreed to move back into her old room.

Antonio had expected Rissa to want the gardens and estate to look 'pretty' as soon as possible. Instead, he'd had to hide his surprise when she'd told him to concentrate his entire workforce on the house. His expression had become unreadable as she'd stressed the urgent need to get two suites habitable as soon as possible. It had only been when Rissa had explained her priorities that his inscrutable expression had slipped—if only for a moment. One apartment would be for her aunt and uncle, the other would be proper staff accommodation for Livia.

'I can manage in these rooms for now,' she'd told him as they stood in the middle of her bare but now clean dressing room. 'As long as all the plumbing and electrics have been renewed by the time my family come and live here.'

The fleeting astonishment in his eyes had made her laugh at the time. Those eyes took on more meaning in the long, lonely hours of darkness. Thinking of Antonio each night was a dangerous occupation. His eyes were always full of such a liquid longing that they haunted Rissa more effectively than talk of any curse. She could imagine him whispering to her through the night, trapping her in the intensity of his gaze while she was helpless beneath the firm, experienced touch of his fingers...

She leapt out of bed. This was ridiculous! Snapping on the light, she pulled on her robe, tying its belt tightly around her slender waist. What was the least sexy thing she could think about? A hot drink, of course...and all those ranks of intense family portraits hanging around the great hall downstairs.

Rissa had been a mousy little thing until her adoptive parents had persuaded her to go to university. It had only really been on her trip to America after her studies that she'd begun to learn that the world was not such a frightening place after all, and that most people were much less alarming than they at first appeared.

Luigi Alfere-Tiziano had fallen into that category, she

thought as she crept around the kitchen, trying to find her precious imported teabags without disturbing Livia. Rissa had been dazzled by Luigi's good looks and charm long before she'd learned that he was rich and titled. In fact, it was the Alfere-Tiziano fortune that had come between them. Luigi's wild extravagance had always made Rissa nervous. As things turned out, she had been right to worry. Her husband's wealth had given him the privilege of endless credit and many servants, most of whom he had treated like dirt.

Rissa sat down on an oaken settle drawn up beside the enormous fireplace. The grate was empty and cold, but there must be plenty of dead, dry wood lying around the estate. She could not wait to see some glittering action in the hearth. Until then, she had to rely on her imagination to provide a roaring fire, crackling away in front of her. Snuggling down, she wrapped her fingers around her steaming mug of tea.

She gazed up at the portraits on the opposite wall. They looked rather better in harsh electric light. Daylight cast more shadows, making their faces seem particularly angular and severe. Something had already struck Rissa as odd about those pictures. Although the many different faces resembled each other, all sharing the same large, dark eyes and aristocratic features, none of the Tiziano family looked remotely like Luigi. Now she came to look around the room, something else was puzzling, too. The huge, ceremonial coat of arms that almost filled the chimney breast. She could not work out the motto, but it definitely included the word 'Michaeli'. Rissa had never heard either Luigi or his mother use it, and it made her wonder why. Luigi's family had been so grand, she was surprised they hadn't quoted their motto at every opportunity.

Rissa thought she could guess the reason why they'd kept

quiet about it. The Alfere-Tizianos had been so autocratic that they'd rarely stooped to acknowledge females. 'Michaeli' was probably the surname of some poor, unsuspecting girl like her, drafted in 'to widen the gene pool', as Luigi had used to put it. Rissa could imagine that once the Tiziano family had laid claim to her possessions and got their precious male heir, she would have been pushed into the background.

Rissa hoped the girl had been luckier than she had. At least a child would have been some consolation for Luigi. He had been eaten up with disappointment, and she had felt so guilty. Then again, she shuddered, pity the poor baby afflicted with a couple like *them* as its parents. Luigi and Rissa had found coping with the paparazzi hard enough. Photos of their child would have filled the glossy magazines, especially when it cried or took fright or otherwise did not behave according to the strict code of the Alfere-Tiziano family.

Two days without sleep began to catch up on Rissa. Her eyelids became heavy. Only the hard oak bench kept her awake. At last she stood up and set off for bed. She took one last look around at the 'rogues gallery' before switching off the lights.

All those faces *were* oddly familiar. If only she could think why…

Sunlight was streaming through the windows of her room when she opened her eyes next morning. Alarmed that it must be late, Rissa sat up. Then she realised something else beside the sunshine had woken her. There was a lot of movement going on downstairs in the kitchen. She went to investigate, and found Livia mopping the floor while Fabio the cat stared out truculently from a refuge in the chimney corner.

'*Scusi, signora*. I was about to bring you a cup of coffee when I tripped over Fabio and almost fell, dropping the cup as I did so.'

'Don't worry about it.' Rissa waved the housekeeper's apology aside. 'Are *you* all right? That is the main thing,' she said with relief, when Livia nodded. 'I never normally sleep so late, so you did me a favour by waking me.'

'No, I didn't, Contessa. I have bad news. I was coming to tell you that I must make an extra visit to the village, so you will be alone here for a while. There was a power cut in the early hours of the morning, so no bread was ready when I first went to the shops.'

'It's on again now, though, isn't it?' Rissa indicated the bare lightbulb, suspended above the kitchen table by a long length of fraying flex.

'Oh, yes, *signora*. I was going to set off as soon as I had taken you your coffee.'

'No—I'll go instead, Livia. I need some exercise to clear my head after waking up in such a hurry,' Rissa volunteered quickly.

She was also glad of an excuse to do some exploring, and possibly meet her neighbours. After a quick shower, she dressed in a tiny striped top and some hip-hugging jeans.

It was a ten-minute walk down into the village. There were no signs that the thunderstorm earlier in the week had ever happened. Rissa's sandals kicked up little puffs of dust as she walked down the track that was all that remained of the *palazzo*'s great drive. Now greenery pressed in on every side as nature tried to reclaim the land. Swifts screamed high in the sky, not low overhead as they did when rain was on the way.

Rissa hesitated when she reached the big gates that opened out into the village square. She was not so confident that she could step straight out into the street. Straightening her top, she sleeked down her hair with nervous hands and cleared her throat. If anyone spoke to her, she did not want to reply with a squeak.

Opening the door a fraction, she was about to take an exploratory peep when she remembered Luigi's scorn at her nervousness. *That is not the way a true Alfere-Tiziano behaves,* he would have said.

That was enough to stiffen her resolve. Taking a deep breath, she plunged straight out into the world beyond the estate.

Monte Piccolo's village square was full of people discussing the recent power cut, and stocking up in case there should be another one. They were all so absorbed that no one took any notice of Rissa. She did not mind. She was happy to slip through the throng almost unnoticed, apart from an occasional watchful nod. Returning the smiles, she moved easily between the crowds.

It was market day, and Rissa toured all the stalls. She chose brown speckled eggs from one great pannier lined with straw, a loaf of bread, and a flat pad of focaccia. She was heading for a stall advertising fresh local fruit and vegetables when she caught sight of Antonio. Her urge to call out to him was stifled when she saw that he was absorbed in animated conversation— with a woman. An extremely beautiful young woman at that.

Rissa took refuge beside the striped side screen of the nearest stall and watched the couple out of the corner of her eye. They were only a few metres away. Rissa could not make out what they were saying, but she did not need to. The impassioned rise and fall of the girl's voice and Antonio's low reassurance sounded suspicious enough. When Rissa plucked up enough courage to glance at them directly, the seductive smile on Antonio's lips as he ran an appreciative hand down the arm of his companion told her this was much more than a simple chat!

Her cheeks burning, Rissa looked away to concentrate on her purchases.

She picked out half a dozen huge beefsteak tomatoes and a selection of salads, then took a chance and looked back at the alcove where Antonio and his 'friend' had been standing. It was deserted. Perhaps he had swept the girl off for a more intimate assignation?

Rissa hardened her heart and told herself that she did not care. It did not stop an invisible hand from clutching at her heart and squeezing tears into the corners of her eyes. Then the unthinkable happened—she heard the low music of Antonio's laughter close at hand. She had to look. Glancing in the direction of the stall she had just left, Rissa saw him. The girl had disappeared, and he was leaning over the colourful display of fruit and vegetables to tease a giggling toddler held in the arms of the stallholder.

He did not seem to have noticed her. Rissa wondered whether or not to go up and speak to him, but he was sharing a joke with one of the locals. It seemed rude to interrupt when he was having a conversation with one of his countrymen. She hesitated, wondering if he would turn and acknowledge her. Then she was suddenly struck by a frightening thought. Suppose he was telling the villagers what he really thought about her? His silky treatment of the unknown girl had shown Rissa that she was not the only one to benefit from his easy manner. What if he was a rat who enticed all women with the same deadly charm, then laughed about it afterwards?

She did not wait to find out. Clutching her purchases, she melted into the crowd before Antonio could look round.

CHAPTER FOUR

'WHERE are you living?' Rissa asked Antonio later that day. They were discussing plans for the refurbishment over Livia's tomato and basil salad.

'Not far away. Over there.' He broke off a piece of focaccia and used it to gesture in the general direction of the Arno.

'I thought you were going to be living in the site office?'

He nodded. 'I might, but at the moment men are trooping in and out all the time. I value my privacy. Projects soon take on a life of their own, and it will become quieter, but for now I prefer to keep myself removed from my workforce.'

Rissa put her head on one side. 'But not the locals?'

'That is the beauty of living in anonymous lodgings.' He ignored the lilt of curiosity in her voice, concentrating instead upon his meal. 'I prefer to rent rooms where no one knows me. That way it is easy enough to dip in and out of company as and when I please. It can be impossible to escape from other people when you live amongst them permanently.'

'You are so right,' Rissa agreed with feeling. 'Mind you, I need a designer dress shop urgently. The faster I can get into Florence at the moment, the better.'

Antonio fixed her with the indulgent smile she had seen him play over the unknown girl earlier that morning.

'Ah…the beautiful Contessa does not need to gild herself on my account. I find her irresistible enough as it is,' he murmured, and then cursed himself silently. The girl was smiling at the touch of his flirtation, but he had intended to make her do all the running. He was pretty sure she must have seen him with Donna that morning. Now she would think he was nothing more than a gigolo, and that was not his intention at all. He wanted credibility.

Rissa was rebuking herself too. Antonio's flattery made her light-headed, despite confirming what she'd already suspected about his true nature. But then, she had been sensible all her life, and where had it got her? She was alone and lonely in a foreign country, without enough money to get back to England, and saddled with a house that would be eating money until she could think of some way of making a living out of it. The only reckless thing she had ever done in her life was to accept Luigi's offer of dinner, five long years ago, and look where *that* had led!

She knew she must be sensible and quash Antonio's attentions straight away, but that was her mind talking. Her body was growing increasingly rebellious. Antonio was clearly the kind of man who would come on to any woman, Rissa told herself. She knew that his type would run a mile from any sort of commitment—unless, like Luigi, they were under pressure to produce a legitimate heir. She knew it was wrong, knew she'd get hurt, but she couldn't deny the intensity of her attraction to him.

'I'm glad you approve of my appearance,' she said, before common sense could stop her. Then she blushed and looked down at her plate, shocked by her own words.

Antonio stopped and gazed at her. After her fine speech about keeping the old Alfere traditions alive, he had begun to have second thoughts about her. Perhaps she might be the first titled woman he had known to break the mould, but, no, she was exactly the same as all the rest. The self-styled Contessa Alfere-Tiziano was no snow maiden, but a red-hot sure thing. That blush could not deny it, he marvelled as he watched the hard points of her nipples rise to thrust against the thin cotton of her blouse. She was aroused, and so, Antonio had to acknowledge, was he.

Rissa was burning with a mixture of guilt and desire. I have got to get back on track before things get out of hand, she realised. If I don't, Livia might return to find us making unusual use of her kitchen table!

She could think of only one way to cool her passion, and that was by speaking out. 'I should not let your pretty little friend down in the village hear you talking like that, Antonio.'

It certainly brought him up short. There had been a smoky, after-dark quality to her voice, which turned his desire for her into a pounding ache. His body fought against common sense. Antonio had proved to himself yet again that the Contessa was the worst example of her type, picking up social inferiors for fun. By rights, he should have nothing to do with her beyond his work on the *palazzo*. Donna had told him that the girl had cast her spell on Mazzini. The land agent had been using Donna as arm-candy for months now, but Antonio knew *that* wouldn't stop a woman like the Contessa moving in to squeeze a rich old suitor until his pips squeaked. Antonio had seen it all too often. No wonder Donna was looking to him for sympathy now.

Rissa took a deep breath. There was nothing for it but to

soften the truth with some cautious talk. 'I need the security of knowing I've always got plenty to fall back on, Antonio. Selling off some of my designer clothes should bring in good money. If this project is to get off the ground, I don't want it to be tied down by cash-flow problems.'

Rissa felt the savage heat of her passion almost instantly transformed into burning shame. Thinking about the sad state of her bank balance always concentrated her mind, and it had worked as well as ever. She could only hope that Antonio did not guess the real reason why she was forced to sell her clothes.

'Hmm.' Antonio picked up his pen and did a few calculations on the pad beside him. Then he sat back in his seat. 'I cannot pretend that this will be a cheap, easy project. The *palazzo* is going to take a great deal of money, Contessa. It is not merely the cost of supplies. There is also the matter of paying the workforce. And the services of Signor Mazzini are expensive, I suppose, especially when he has a high-maintenance mistress like Donna to support. She is the creature you saw me with in the market,' he added, in an off-hand manner.

'That is why I must realise some of my assets, Antonio.'

'At least I am working for free.'

'I haven't forgotten, and I'm very grateful,' Rissa said firmly.

'Mind you, I could always become your own, personal, tax-deductible expense—' he laughed wryly, but Rissa stopped him with a horrified gasp as Livia bustled into the room.

'No—no—I am sure that won't be necessary!' she said hurriedly, never quite certain when he was serious and when he might be joking.

'Do not worry, Contessa. For the greater glory of a place like the Palazzo Tiziano, I am glad to work for nothing,' he said with a knowing smile.

* * *

During her marriage, Rissa had become used to living in luxury. It had been a false paradise, but a very comfortable one. Abandoned in a Manhattan duplex, she had been brought out only for the grandest social occasions, spells in the Hamptons, or trips on the Alfere-Tiziano yacht. She had experienced gracious living, but her time had been dictated by the social calendar.

Things would be very different at the Palazzo Tiziano, Rissa realised as she stepped out onto the upper terrace next day. Antonio had gone into town to organise electricians and plumbers, but even when the utilities had been sorted out Rissa knew the house would still look stark and sad. There would be precious little comfort for her beyond her own suite.

Thinking of her bedroom instantly conjured up Antonio's image again, so Rissa quickly concentrated on making another circuit of the estate. An idea had been forming in her mind ever since she had caught part of Antonio's conversation with the old stallholder yesterday morning in the market. When she had asked him about it, Antonio had been only too willing to give her more details.

It turned out that the market gardener's only son had a good office job in Florence, and had no intention of carrying on his family's tradition of working on the land. The elderly stallholder wanted to retire, and would have to close the stall down. The fruit and vegetables were so popular with Livia and other villagers that Rissa knew its loss would be significant. Italians loved fresh, homegrown food, and although Rissa had no money for creature comforts at the Palazzo Tiziano, she had lots of land. She knew from tours with Antonio that her estate already grew pine nuts, almonds, figs, grapes and apricots. Sadly, fallen fruits enjoyed only by insects sur-rounded the untended trees and bushes.

As she walked carefully around her property now she could see more possibilities. Wild strawberries grew in cracks between paving stones. If they could manage in such poor places, how much better would they grow in a proper plot of good rich soil? Large, saleable berries from cultivated plants were sure to find a ready market in the village. Rissa worked her way towards the far boundary of her estate, where the old *campanile* stood like a pointing finger. *It is a beautiful building*, she realised, stopping to admire the vine-covered tower. Although it was clearly not in good condition, Antonio had been to the top without coming to any harm. All the dangerous areas around the place were marked off with striped tape and cones now—that had been one of his first jobs. The campanile had no warnings, so it could not be in *that* bad a state. Surely she could take a quick look inside?

The idea of having a fling with Antonio has opened my mind to all sorts of risky things. Rissa smiled as she walked up to the wooden door. She had already decided that the tower would be an ideal setting for a café, with views out over the grounds. Her adoptive parents only had window boxes back in England, but they looked on a trip to their local garden centre as a special outing. If they could have tea and cakes while they were out, that counted as a real treat. Rissa knew that by appealing to the villagers' enjoyment of coffee and chatting, as well as their desire for good fresh produce, she might provide herself with an income.

Reaching the *campanile*'s door, she paused and looked around. There was no one about. She picked up the great iron ring that served as a handle and immediately caught the tang of lubricant. The door was dry, and cracked with age, but its handle turned smoothly enough. Pushing it open, she peered into the shadowy interior.

Rissa had expected rubble, dead leaves, and perhaps some pigeon feathers. To her surprise, the spacious interior was clean and tidy. A notebook, clipboard, pen and large surveyor's tape measure lay on a far windowsill. Someone was already hard at work somewhere.

'Antonio?' she called, making her way to the staircase that must lead up to the bell tower. There was no reply. Gingerly starting up the steps, she put her hand to the wooden banister, which creaked menacingly. Rissa felt unsafe. She was about to retrace her steps and creep back out into the grounds when a sudden clatter made her jump. Grabbing for the stair rail, she felt it dissolve into powder beneath her hands and lost her balance. With a scream, she fell crashing to the ground.

Firm, authoritative hands were running over her body. Rissa tried to rouse herself, but her head was pounding and her throat was dry with dust. She was powerless. There was nothing she could do but lie still in the half-light and submit to a fingertip examination of each of her limbs in turn.

'Antonio!' she managed at last.

'Shh. You have had a nasty fall, Contessa. Do not move until I have checked thoroughly to make sure you are OK. Do you make a habit of tumbling to the feet of every man you meet?'

There was a low chuckle behind his voice, but it was his hands that concerned her. They moved with practised ease over her body. His slow, measured movements were almost a caress as they glided across her skin. In the silence, Rissa closed her eyes again. As Antonio's examination ran across her ribcage an involuntary gasp escaped from her lips.

'Was that painful?'

He bent so close that the stimulating male tang of him was almost a taste on her tongue. Her body began to respond, making her catch her breath again.

'You are in pain?' His voice was almost a purr, as though he expected her to make the most of the situation.

'No—ouch! Well, only from this lump on my head,' she winced.

'Let me see.'

Sliding his hands beneath her shoulders, he drew her gently into a sitting position. His face was now only millimetres away from hers.

'Look into my eyes, Contessa.'

It was hypnotism. Rissa was trapped in the deep, dark depths of those brown eyes. With a little gasp her lips parted, and she moistened them with the tip of her tongue, already imagining that she could feel the pressure of him taking possession of her mouth. Her fingers clenched convulsively and she found that she was gripping his arm. With a shock, she sprang back to reality. What a position to be in! Blushing, she scrambled away from him, desperate to hide her humiliation.

As he stood up, Antonio too had something to conceal.

'There cannot be much wrong with you if you can move like that!' He forced a chuckle, but his voice was low with testosterone. The fact was that Rissa was having a disturbing effect on him.

His plan had been to get his house back, with or without seducing her—it had not mattered much to him either way. This was to have been an emotionless business venture, completely free from the entanglement of feelings. Antonio could deal with basic sex. That gave him no problems at all. It was this sudden urgency of real desire, ravening need, which grew and consumed him with a fire of longing the type of which he had never known before. When he had felt her pliant body responding to his touch, he had been almost overwhelmed with the urge to take her right there, to move his body even closer to hers than he was to his own, to—

She slipped past him and was gone. Brushing dust from the knees of his jeans, Antonio followed her out of the building and into the sunlight.

'If that place is unsafe it should have a sign on the door.' Rissa rubbed the bruise on her head as they walked round to begin surveying the outside of the main building.

'It was perfectly safe until you decided to go exploring, Contessa. Most of the ground floor is good enough to use as extra storage space for supplies. It is *not* suitable for casual visitors.' He finished sternly. 'Now, if you stand on the bottom rung of this ladder, I shall go up and investigate the state of the upper facings of the house.'

'It was the clatter you made dropping this wretched thing that made me lose my balance,' Rissa said as she watched him advancing up the steps towards a clear blue sky.

'If you had not been poking around in a place that I had already told you was not totally safe, Contessa, your guilty conscience would not have made you jump like a frightened rabbit.'

'It seems such a waste of a good building. One day it ought to be made into extra living space.'

'I hope you are not suggesting that it should become another holiday home?' he said gruffly. 'Property and rental prices in the village are astronomical because of them. Young people cannot marry easily, because houses are so expensive here. When wed, they often start life together by living with their parents. No developer could be bothered to build cheap homes in Monte Piccolo. There is little work here, so it is executive houses and holiday apartments that make all the money. The only hope for young people today is to move away from pretty villages like this.'

'I might be able to help with some of that, at least,' Rissa said. 'The *palazzo* can provide jobs. Could you make sure you employ as many people from the village as possible, Antonio? It would at least give them some chance of making money without leaving home.'

'OK, but only if you are prepared to give proper contracts of employment and legal rates of pay. There must be no under-the-table deals for cash. I will not trade on their desperation,' he warned.

'It will all be arranged properly, through Signor Mazzini.'

Antonio shrugged. 'That won't please him. He prefers to employ his friends from town. If I choose the workers, Mazzini won't have any control over them. Are you willing to upset your gentleman friend like that, Contessa?'

'Signor Mazzini is not my "gentleman friend", as you put it. In any case, I thought you said that woman you were talking to in the market place was his girlfriend?'

'They have a casual arrangement, Contessa. Are you jealous?' Antonio came down the ladder and snapped his pencil back into its holder on top of his clipboard. 'Although this will take your mind off romance—it looks as though the Palazzo Tiziano needs a whole new roof. That will not come cheap. You should be more concerned about that than with other people's love-lives.'

Rissa shook her head in bewilderment. 'It needs a new roof? Signor Mazzini didn't say anything about that!'

'He did not have to, Contessa. You were inheriting the old place, not buying it.'

'How much is it likely to cost, exactly?'

She was looking worried. Antonio raised his eyebrows. Trying to scare her out of the house with old wives' tales had not worked. Perhaps this different set of thumbscrews might do the trick. Rich women liked to spend on luxuries, not property maintenance. Sticking his hands in his pockets, he rocked back on his heels, pursing his lips. He studied the façade of the once grand house for a long time before replying.

'Hmm. The new work must match what it replaces. Flashings and coving and ridge tiles must be cast and cut to match the original work. Master craftsmen will need to be employed, and maintained on site for as long as it takes. We are talking about a great deal of money, Contessa.'

'How much?' Rissa probed nervously.

'That is impossible to pin down, but big money, certainly.'

She heaved a huge sigh.

Antonio tore his gaze away from the beautiful old house and regarded her keenly. 'Look—may I speak frankly, Contessa?'

'You might as well. Whatever you say cannot possibly make my situation any worse, can it?' she muttered.

His mouth almost twitched into a grin. 'In my opinion, the old place is not worth your while. You don't have to put yourself through all this stress, Contessa. Why don't you sell up and go back to your people in England?'

Rissa folded her arms, hugging herself against the chill draught of financial disaster. 'You *know* why, Antonio. You have said as much yourself. A rich developer would snap this place up at a fraction of its historical and real value. One of them was sniffing around within days of my husband's accident. There are wolves everywhere! They would either knock the *palazzo* down completely, or make it into expensive flats. Whatever they did, these beautiful grounds would be lost for ever under acres of concrete, parking spaces and the designer homes you yourself were so scornful about not long ago.'

She was turning his own words back on him. Antonio considered them. What she had said was true enough, but he knew there must be some deeper reasoning behind it. Women always liked to keep men guessing. It was the way they worked—they preferred to keep their prey off-balance. There would be some other motive for the Contessa wanting to keep the Palazzo Tiziano.

Antonio led the way around to the back of the house. He was deep in thought. His company, AMI Holdings, had made such generous offers for the whole estate that anyone in their right mind would have taken the money and blessed their luck. His people back in Cardiff, and the staff of Mazzini's office in Florence, had all agreed that the Contessa would be mad to turn it down. Then Mazzini himself had stepped in to block the first offer. The Contessa had refused the increased figure. She seemed to prefer scraping a bare living here rather than cutting her losses and heading back home.

Antonio had to know if there really was anything between her and Enrico Mazzini. Secure in the knowledge that no unattached woman could resist him, he decided to put her to the test.

The house had been developed over the centuries. Additions to one end of its main building had created a private, sunny area, sheltered on three sides, but open to the south.

'This would be perfect for sunbathing,' he said, treading down the dry grass that had been left to grow untended for years.

'And the weather is exactly right for it today, too.' Rissa joined him in padding the greenery down into a soft bed.

'Then be my guest, Contessa!'

Rissa laughed. 'I'd have to go back into the house and fetch some lotion. Then the moment would be gone. I would find too many jobs to do before I could get out here again!'

'Then let me fetch some for you. This spot is completely secluded, and the men are all working on the other side of the house. You can strip off and stretch out in privacy.' He was looking at her so innocently that Rissa was struck with sudden devilment.

'All right—I shall! There is a bottle on top of the cabinet in the kitchen, Antonio.' She put a hand to one strap of her sundress, but stopped when she saw that he was still watching.

He took the hint and walked off with a smile. A pleasure delayed would be double the fun. In seconds he had retrieved the sun lotion, but did not go straight back outside. Instead he took the stairs two at a time and went into Rissa's suite. It overlooked the sheltered quadrangle, giving Antonio his own private view of the grass below.

The girl must have lost her nerve. She had not stripped off, but was lying face down on the grass in her sundress. All her most interesting features were still hidden from Antonio, but despite that he felt himself rising to the challenge. Her smooth, slender limbs and the gentle curve of her back were meant for his caress. He turned away from the window and strode off to put his fantasies into action.

Stealthy as a panther, he padded across the grass, taking care that his shadow did not disturb her. Even so, she sensed his arrival and began to raise herself on one elbow. It was too late. Silhouetted against the sun, he was pouring sun tan lotion into the palm of one hand.

'Lie down,' he commanded. It was not a voice to be questioned. Rissa heard him snap the bottle closed and tensed. He noticed.

'This is no good. You must relax to get all the benefit of this sun, Contessa.'

'Yes, but I'm not altogether sure that this is—'

The firm strokes of Antonio's hands running over her shoulders stifled any objections.

His lips twitched with the hint of a smile. 'Contessa, explain to me how you are supposed to apply this stuff all on your own!'

Rissa felt him take long sweeping strokes up her neck and down her arms. She knew he must be kneeling astride her, but he was taking care that no part of his body touched hers apart from his swirling, massaging hands. Suddenly his movements stopped. She expected to hear the bottle being opened again. Instead, the halter neck of her sundress was unfastened. She gasped as it fell away, leaving her back completely exposed.

'As soon as I leave you will wriggle out of it, so why take the risk of leaving the skin beneath your straps unprotected?' His fingers spread a slick of lotion over her shoulderblades.

Rissa closed her eyes, revelling in the half-forgotten feeling of a man's hands running over her body. She knew she should call a halt, but part of her—something buried deep inside—made her want him to continue, even to risk going further…

He did not. Instead, she heard him pour out more cream. This time he moved back and began oiling her calves. When he progressed beneath the hem of her dress, Rissa gave a deep, heartfelt sigh.

'That is good, isn't it?' Antonio was enjoying himself hugely. The contrast between his rough workman's palms and her soft skin gave him a delicious foretaste of pleasures to come.

'Mmm.'

He flattened his hands against her thighs, making swimming movements that went up and around, up and around, higher and higher, until the tips of his fingers brushed beneath the elastic of her panties. The intrusion met with no resistance, so as smoothly as ever Antonio continued, each circuit taking him a little further into the forbidden zone. When those tactics brought his palms fully into contact with her bare behind, he could resist no longer. His smooth strokes changed to a cupping, squeezing motion.

'No!' she warned him firmly, but not before he had heard a little moan wander between her parted lips.

'Why? Because you do not like it?'

She liked it very much, but in this situation honesty would be her downfall. To put a stop to it would confirm what Luigi had always thought about her, but then *he* had never made her body respond as Antonio did. Rissa tried to dodge the issue.

'It isn't that.'

'What is it, then? Don't tell me you are afraid of what people might think? That is the worst reason of all, at any time and in any place.' Antonio leaned forward until his breath caressed her shoulder. 'The *palazzo* is empty. None of the workers has my permission to come around to this part of the building, and my word is law.' With the last word he kissed the delicate skin beneath her ear.

The touch of his lips released a shiver of anticipation that coursed through her body. Reality slipped away. Rissa melted beneath his hands as they ran along the length of her body, still slick with lotion. Squirming beneath him, she twisted like a seal, desperate to escape but equally desperate for him to continue stroking her body. The strange new feeling suddenly threw a switch in Rissa's head. *I can't do this*, she thought. *If I go any further Antonio will find out. He will discover the horrible truth about me and I couldn't bear it.*

'Stop!' A coiled spring of fear and desperation, she hit him a glancing blow. He leapt away, equally horrified. Clutching at her dress, Rissa crouched in the grass like a fawn at bay. Antonio blacked out the sun. As he approached she saw that his dark eyes were turbulent, and his hands were balled into fists.

'I—I don't want this, Antonio. I never intended you to go as far as you did.'

His stare was cruel with disbelief. She could not meet it, and shut her eyes against her shame and his fury. When he spoke, his voice was low and dangerous.

'No. That is a lie. You were as willing as I was, Contessa. But then the truth kicked in. You got cold feet. You began to think that your Signor Mazzini might dump you if he thought you had been playing around with your staff.'

His first few words were true enough, but the rest was a lie. Rissa agonised to herself. There was no way she could tell Antonio the true reason why she had called a halt. The fact was that, despite her marriage, she was still inexperienced in the ways of love. A man like Antonio would be sure to take advantage of that.

'No, Antonio—Mazzini means nothing to me. And as for the rest…you've got it all wrong…' Her voice faded as she saw the cynicism in his smile.

'I don't think so, Contessa. Your idea is to keep me sweet, and then perhaps I'll help you out still further by arranging some favourable cash terms for the building materials you need. Isn't that the way you are thinking?'

Rissa's dealings with Mazzini had shown her that the black economy worked in the same way the world over. He always quoted two figures for any transaction—one for cash, and one to go through the books. Rissa insisted on paying the correct amount for everything. Mazzini kept suggesting that everyone had his or her price, but she had been unwilling to believe it. Now here was Antonio, expecting her to be wise in all the ways of fiddling expenses and manipulating her workforce.

'This has nothing to do with any of that,' she muttered, but he had already made up his mind.

'Of course it does. A rich woman without a man is never satisfied. Then along comes wealthy old Mazzini. I am sure you can wind him around your little finger. You need to get the *palazzo* up and running, but you haven't yet managed to get your hands on his credit card. My offer to work for nothing must have seemed like a gift from the gods! In your world, Contessa, nobody does anything for nothing. Perhaps you were feeling a little guilty, eh? You were expecting a poor peasant like me to be overawed by the attentions of the lady of the manor. When I proved to be more than equal to the task, you pulled back.' He was looking down on her with undisguised contempt.

Rissa was in agony. She already knew what it was like to have her self-esteem trampled underfoot. Luigi's unspoken disappointment in her had tortured Rissa often enough. But that was nothing compared to the pain Antonio was inflicting on her now. Humiliation was burning in her face and forming an insoluble lump in her throat. A moment ago she had almost lost control beneath his hands, exposing herself in a way that she had never risked before. To learn that her reaction had fulfilled some kind of terrible expectation in him was a thousand times worse than all the old taunts put together.

'You don't understand, Antonio! I'm not like that!' she burst out when the pain became unendurable. He gave a mirthless laugh.

'So I imagined it—you *didn't* make the first move? I think you did, Contessa. I felt your body come to life beneath my hands. And when I responded in kind, I found you were as hot and willing as any woman I have ever known—'

'No!' Instinctively Rissa responded with all the pain of wounded pride, but he was quicker. With the speed of a striking snake he grabbed her wrist before her hand could connect with his cheek again.

'When the truth hurts, try to silence it, eh?' He grinned, his fingers biting into the thin skin of her inner arm. 'That is the way women like you work, isn't it?'

Rissa looked at him, horrified. He laughed.

'No, you might have pushed me to the edge, Contessa, but unlike some men I have no intention of pressing my advantage.'

'Then let go of me!' She managed to stop her voice rising to a scream, but it was a struggle. His grip was relentless and his eyes poured darkness into her. 'Any meeting I may have with Signor Mazzini is only for the good of the Palazzo Tiziano. You have no right to suggest anything else!'

She had to swallow hard to stop tears of panic and inner pain from rising up and choking her, but she was not about to break down in front of him. 'My first and only thoughts are always to do the best for this house.'

'Don't give me that! Your sort are always quick to play the old honour card.'

'And what exactly *is* my "sort"?'

'You are a typical member of the monied classes, Contessa. When they are down on their luck, they are always quick to hitch a ride on the lifeboat of new money. You had a fine meal ticket in the shape of Luigi Alfere. When you lost that, it was time to find another. Along comes the portly, vain Signor Mazzini, and you are set up for life again. Well, congratulations—you could hardly have made a better choice. The man is old and unfit—with any luck you won't have to suffer his attentions for too long before you wear him out. Then you'll move on to some other rich provider—anything to stop you having to fend for yourself. You are a leaner, Contessa. You lean on people to get what you want, always relying on someone else to come up with the goods.'

'No! I won't listen to this!' Growing hysteria lent Rissa the strength to rip her arm from his grasp and turn her back on him as she did up her sundress. 'You know nothing about my circumstances. Nobody—especially not a man who comes across like an over-sexed dinosaur when it comes to women—speaks to me like that. Especially on my own land!' she announced. But he was already striding away around the corner of the house.

Rissa was as taut as a bowstring all the way to her room, listening for the sound of Antonio in case he decided to seek her out again. It never came. Only when she had retreated behind locked doors did she collapse onto the edge of her new bed and bury her face in her hands. How could Antonio be so utterly wrong about her—especially when she had been so right about him? On that first dark night she had sensed instantly that he was all man. Why, then, had *he* misjudged *her* so badly? She had always fallen outside the circle of well-to-do women who ran the social life of Manhattan. That didn't stop her recognising the picture Antonio had painted of idle privilege. But she was different—wasn't she?

She knew how those women would have reacted to that kind of treatment from a man like Antonio. He would have been thrown off the premises without a reference. Rissa would have done the same. But three things stopped her. One—Antonio galvanised everyone into action as soon as they became involved in the *palazzo* project. They were only a few days into the work, but things were already happening on a grand scale. Two—he was working for no wages. At least, that had been the arrangement when they'd last spoken civilly about the matter. And last—but in Rissa's mind most importantly of all—he had taught her a vital lesson. Her body was not the lifeless thing of marble that marriage to Luigi had led her to believe.

She had thought the fault was on her side, but now she was beginning to wonder. Given the right stimulation, she could respond like the most hot-blooded, passionate of women, and Antonio had reacted accordingly. Every time she looked at him, she was playing with fire. Giving in to temptation was only a touch away. *Well, I shan't be burning my fingers,* she told herself. *Antonio has done me a favour by destroying any fantasies I may have had about him. His reality is too painful. I won't be going there again,* she thought, still burning with humiliation when she remembered how he saw her. He had said that she was a woman on the make, no different from any other. It was such a painful jibe that tears of outrage sprang to her eyes. Rissa rubbed them away in fury. She had thought her defences against the world were so good that no one—especially no man—would ever be able to breach them.

Antonio was the only one who had come close to breaking down her resolve. She vowed then and there that he must never again come so close to discovering her painful secret.

CHAPTER FIVE

RISSA knelt outside the great front doors of the Palazzo Tiziano, her radio playing by her side. She was weeding, shaded from the heat by a broad-brimmed straw hat. Every crevice around the big old house was green with weeds. She might not be able to re-tile a roof or use an angle grinder, but she could at least work to make the place look a bit more presentable.

In the days since Antonio had compared her to the idle women of his acquaintance, she had found a million things to do. They all involved keeping her head down, as far away from him as possible. She had been working from morning until night to stop her mind dwelling on what had happened.

It was now almost midday, and Rissa had been on her hands and knees since five o'clock that morning. She had made so many trips to empty her pail of weeds that she had lost count. The work was hard. Only the memory of Antonio's taunts that day about the lazy society she had left behind kept her going. Rissa was determined to show him that she was totally unlike those other women. Besides, if she took a back seat and did nothing towards restoring the Palazzo Tiziano, she really would be in Antonio's debt. She hated the thought of obligation like that. It was bad enough to know that the *palazzo* was such a drain on her rapidly vanishing finances.

She sat back on her heels and looked up at the fine, creamy stonework of the building's façade. Blank windows gazed out over the rolling Tuscan countryside. Rissa bit her lip. Curtains behind all that flawed glass would cheer the place up instantly, but no money could be spared for luxuries like that. Then she had an idea. A few old rose bushes were still clinging to life in the wilderness of the estate. Their willowy growth could spare armfuls of flowers for the house.

Brushing gritty soil off her hands, Rissa stood up. She looked down proudly at what she had achieved. A large area of the courtyard was now looking neat and presentable. She was overdue a break in which to do something nicer. Fetching some scissors from the kitchen, she set off, and within ten minutes had filled her weeding bucket with wands of sweet-smelling flowers. As well as roses, she had found sprays of myrtle, rosemary and arbutus, to make a special arrangement for her bedside. There was no point in living in such splendour if she could not enjoy it indoors as well as out.

As she carried her prizes around the corner of the house, she walked straight into Antonio. He must be the only man who can make overalls and a hard hat look sexy, she thought, and blushed.

He looked pointedly at her container of flowers. 'Where have you been? Livia wants to serve lunch. There are plenty more jobs around here that are more important than picking flowers.'

'I have spent all morning on my hands and knees clearing the terrace!' Rissa bridled indignantly.

'I know. But, as I say, if you want to make yourself useful, there are more urgent tasks that need tackling first.'

'The front of this house is pretty important to me. And, as I am sure you would be the first to point out, Antonio, I am totally unskilled labour.' Rissa stood with one hand on her hip, daring Antonio to contradict her.

'I know, so I have thought of a job that even you can do, Contessa. All the exterior paintwork needs to be stripped off the ground floor of the main house. That will be your task this afternoon, once you have had your food. The sun will be away from the front of the building by then. Have you ever used a blowtorch?' He grinned, knowing he was right to be scornful. This delicate little Contessa might dabble with cosmetic touches, like weeding or flower arranging, but when it came down to real work she would be sure to disappear without a trace.

'No, I haven't—but if you could spare some time to teach me, I could learn.'

This was not the reply Antonio had expected, but he rallied instantly. 'You'll have to be careful not to crack the glass, Contessa. Perhaps if I tell you that it costs twelve euros to replace each of those small panes, it will inspire you not to break any.'

It did, but Rissa was not about to let Antonio think his instructions had intimidated her.

She did not hurry her lunch. Then she arranged displays of flowers in several of the downstairs windows at the front of the building before strolling off to find her instructor.

'My employees will not be impressed if you use all their containers for foliage, Contessa,' Antonio said, as he filled a workman's trug with a blowtorch and scrapers.

'I only used a couple of their buckets. There were some old vases in a cupboard,' she countered, shivering at the thought of all the cobwebs that had been hidden away in there as well. 'Now—what about all this desperately important work you want me to do?'

Antonio was wary of underestimating Rissa a second time. He took great care to teach her exactly how he wanted the work done.

'You are a quick study,' he said at last, when he could no longer fight against giving the compliment.

'There is no need to sound so grudging.'

'I am a busy man, Contessa. I don't have time for pointless chit-chat.'

'Then don't feel you have to waste any more of your valuable time on me,' she said lightly, peeling a long curl of aged paint off a windowframe with the satisfaction of someone who had found a new vocation in life.

Antonio wasn't about to march off straight away. He had not obeyed any woman since he was fifteen, and he was not about to start now. Strolling away in his own good time, he found himself listening, waiting for her to call him back. When she did not, he went to find comfort in checking up on how things were going back at the headquarters of AMI Holdings.

Reaching the site office, he pulled off his overalls. Then he straightened his shirt and brushed down his jeans before taking his place at the desk. Switching on his laptop, he checked the share prices. Careful growth and continual monitoring meant the market was smiling on AMI Holdings. That was good. His staff would all be in line for another windfall payment at Christmas. Antonio fired off the e-mails that would eventually cascade down through his thousands of workers and sub-contractors. He had interests across Europe and the United States, yet despite his international business,

Antonio was very much a hands-on employer. When his own fortunes rose, he wanted everyone to share in them.

When he had finished on the computer, Antonio allowed himself the luxury of a hot *macciato*. This was one of the perks of his deception. Pulling rank as site manager actually gave him the chance to savour drinks—proper drinks—from beginning to end. When he was working outside, coffee after instant coffee had to be parked and abandoned. If the cups were eventually rediscovered, there was always a thick layer of plaster or dust on the surface of his drink, so Antonio had become used to going thirsty. Today would be different. He had managed to speak with the girl again, after that setback over the sunbathing, so he deserved a reward.

Some of his newer staff might have found it strange that Antonio Michaeli-Isola chose to spend his annual leave working unpaid at the Palazzo Tiziano, but then their boss was an unusual man. He rarely took time off work for any reason, much less holiday. There had been real trouble in his early life, until a teacher at his school had tried to find out the reason behind his truancy.

Old Dini had discovered that Antonio was out earning money when he should have been in the classroom. The boy had felt he had to do something to support his widowed mother and aged grandmother. Antonio's talent for working with his hands had been put to good use. Anyone in the area who had needed jobs done quickly and well had called for him. When his teacher had learned about this, he had persuaded the school's vocational department to hone Antonio's skills.

The boy had repaid all the trust put in him. By the age of nineteen he had earned enough to buy his first derelict property. This had been sold on to a young local couple for an affordable price, though Antonio had still made a good profit on the deal. And now, however high he might fly, he never forgot what it was like to be at a disadvantage. That was why he liked to go back to labouring now and again. Working with his own hands instead of merely issuing orders was Antonio's idea of a good time. To be restoring the Palazzo Tiziano made it a double pleasure. Not only could he take pride in what was being achieved, he knew that sooner or later the place would be his.

He owed it to his ancestors to care for their home. They had lived and loved here since Roman times, certainly, and perhaps even right back to the Etruscans. On the other hand, Antonio felt he owed nothing at all to those pampered upstarts the Alfere family. They had merely got lucky. It was, Antonio supposed, what they called the fortunes of war. He did not intend to be on the losing side *this* time.

As for the Contessa… He thought for a moment, gazing into the middle distance with half-closed eyes. Taking her would be sweet revenge. It would be no more than those treacherous Alferes deserved. There would be a more personal bonus, too. Not only would Antonio be avenging his family's honour, it would serve the Contessa right for leading him on. He was looking forward to enjoying her and righting wrongs at the same time. His workmen always paused to admire the girl as she passed, and that really annoyed him. Not only was she distracting them, it stirred an unexpected mixture of possessiveness and an instinct within Antonio that was disturbingly close to the animal. This did not sit easily with his finer feelings. It aroused him to know that the girl he needed to bed to secure the greatest prize of all—his *palazzo*—was the object of other men's desires. Yet the whole master and mistress thing left a nasty taste in his mouth.

The trouble was, that girl was a thief. She had married into this house, obtaining it under false pretences. Now she showed every sign of wanting to hang on to the place. He sipped his coffee, frowning. She was a burglar of emotions, inspiring a powerful cocktail of feelings within Antonio. Plenty of women could arouse him physically, but the Contessa Alfere-Tiziano also managed to rouse him to anger and seduce him at the same time.

No other woman had ever affected him like this before, and it made him uneasy.

Rissa felt herself fizzing with anticipation as she approached the site office door. She had survived one conversation today with Antonio, but now she was approaching his lair. Confidence in the work she had done for him was making her bold. Gingerly, she tapped on the door. A loud order to 'come in' made her hesitate. It was only for a fraction of a second, but that was too long for Antonio. He pulled the door open to confront his visitor. Dressed in well-cut jeans and a white linen shirt, he was one of those men who showed his style even on a working day.

'Where is your hard hat?' He pointed to a nearby sign. It was one of many dotted all around the busy building site that the estate had become.

'I left it on the front doorstep while I walked over here from the house. It is too hot to wear that thing when I am not working.'

His dark brows contracted. 'It is never too hot to obey the rules of Health and Safety.'

Her face compressed with anger. She spun around on her heel, ready to march off again.

'Wait!' He caught her by the arm.

'I was going back to fetch it.' Rissa glared at his restraining hand. Instantly he let her go. 'I only came over to see if you wanted to inspect the work I have done.'

'This isn't technical college, Contessa. At school, the teacher gives you ten out of ten for decent work. Out here, in the real world, you must take responsibility for yourself. If you are satisfied, then so am I. This is currently your house. I am merely here to make sure things run smoothly and to schedule. *If* I am allowed to get on without interruptions, of course,' he added dryly.

Rissa was about to reply in kind. Then she realised his attention had been snatched away by something else. Turning around, she saw Donna, the dark-haired young woman from the market.

The newcomer was picking her way across the courtyard. Even from a distance she looked wonderful. A white off-the-shoulder lacy top was cut short to show off a strip of flat, bronzed stomach above a pair of hip-hugging Capri pants. A large pair of sunglasses was pushed up on top of her head, holding back a riot of purplish-red curls. As she drew closer, Rissa realised that the stranger's mass of hair had the dry, straw-like texture caused by constant over-processing.

Antonio did not seem to mind. His attention was straying lower down, to where a pair of strangely immobile breasts bulged over the low neckline of Donna's *broderie anglaise* top.

'Antonio—I'm *sooo* glad you are here! I cannot imagine how I would have felt to have struggled all the way up here and then found the place empty!'

Rissa bit back the retort that Antonio was only one of dozens working at the *palazzo*, but it hardly seemed necessary. Donna was ignoring her totally, and had eyes only for Antonio.

'Enrico is having a dinner party this evening. Why don't you join us?'

Antonio smiled briefly. 'I assume your invitation also extends to my client the Contessa, Donna?'

The woman turned a pair of pale blue eyes on Rissa. Twinkling with laughter, she shot a look that dared her to accept.

'Actually, I'm rather busy tonight.' Rissa smiled graciously. As far as she was concerned, stripping paint sounded much more fun than spending hours watching Donna make sheep's eyes at Antonio.

'In which case I would be delighted to accept.' Antonio gave the messenger such a knowing look that it made Rissa blush. Donna merely winked archly and turned on her heel.

'We'll see you at around nine, then, Antonio. *Ciao!*'

'*Ciao,*' he repeated, raising his hand in farewell. For some moments his eyes were fastened on Donna's well-upholstered rear end as it undulated down the drive.

'Your friend might have found it easier on her stilettos to use the telephone,' Rissa observed.

'Yes—although it would not have been such a pleasurable experience. For either of us.' Antonio gave one of his eloquent smiles.

I certainly didn't enjoy it, Rissa fumed as she walked from the site office back to her work on the house. A hard knot of pain was tangling her emotions, confusing her. Antonio was an overbearing misogynist. If that was the kind of man Donna wanted, then she was welcome to him. *I don't need that sort of conflict in my life,* Rissa told herself.

But, if that was the case, why did the sight of Antonio exchanging glances with Donna affect her so much?

Antonio never needed much sleep. Next morning, he was strolling through the grounds of the *palazzo* before the sun had pushed clear of the furthest line of hills. Pencil-thin cypresses were still nothing more than black shapes pointing skywards as he approached the front of his beautiful *palazzo*. He stopped a few metres short of the façade to study its new appearance. The growing daylight was no longer reflecting off ancient white paintwork. All the exposed wood on the ground floor now looked as though it had been ravaged by fire.

Heart in his mouth, Antonio went forward to inspect any damage more closely. There was none. The girl had been careful enough, he admitted grudgingly to himself as he fingered all the mouldings and the *palazzo*'s great double doors.

It really was a beautiful building, set off by ideal surroundings, Antonio thought, casting a critical eye over the cobbled forecourt. The Contessa had done a good job there as well. She had shown vision on their first tours around the gardens, too. The mousy little English girl was displaying hidden depths and talents.

He approached one of the tall windows. Leaning forward, he cupped one hand against the glass to see into the room beyond. Rissa had filled a Lalique vase with roses and put it on a French-polished side table. Antonio noticed that she had placed a tablemat beneath the crystal. That would certainly stop water or the base of her flower arrangement marking what he suspected was a Louis XVI piece. His inspection continued. In her urge to improve the *palazzo*, she must have washed away inches of dust from this room alone. It was one of the best-preserved areas in the whole complex, and she was trying to show it to advantage.

The high walls and carved ceiling had all been cleaned, making the room look even more airy and spacious. It was empty, apart from her flower arrangement and a dustpan and brush standing beside the huge marble fireplace. Antonio began to feel uneasy again. It would not be long before his men were being borrowed to carry out silly, female-inspired tasks like black-leading grates or sanding the floorboards— which looked good enough to take the treatment and then remain on display without carpets, he noted in passing.

Stepping back from the window, Antonio prowled around the rest of the ground floor. Livia was not due to start work for more than an hour, and he suspected that Rissa would not be surfacing at any time soon. She must have toiled long into the evening to achieve so much paint-stripping, he thought with wry amusement. It had probably been an attempt to work off all that sexual frustration.

Eventually, he went over to the site office, let himself in and switched on his laptop. The business side of his brain watched the display of international financial news, but the analytical part of his mind was elsewhere. It was employed in a much more complex problem. The image he had been sold of Larissa Alfere-Tiziano, as the press called her, was that of an airhead who'd got lucky. On that basis, *his* people had made *her* people good offers for the *palazzo*. Antonio's first jolt had been her refusal to sell. Then his confidence had taken a blow when she had not been scared away from the place by either its condition or his tales. If he could neither buy nor frighten her out of this house that was rightfully his, there was surely only one route left. But that business with the suntan lotion had put a dent in those plans, too.

What was wrong with the woman? She had been hot for him, then suddenly the barricades had gone up so fast it was a wonder he hadn't lost his fingers—or something closer to the action! Antonio stroked his chin thoughtfully. She was a woman alone, and had been clearly tempted by the thought of sex with no strings. But when it had come to actually doing it…something had gone wrong. Antonio knew she had the potential to be as much of a sexual being as he was. He had felt it in her response. Her dark, sensuous eyes had been all for him, and that generous mouth had been silently asking to be kissed. Yet she had pulled back at the last moment…

He grimaced at the memory of Enrico Mazzini's dinner party the previous evening. Donna could do with taking some lessons in restraint from the English Contessa. Concealed by the long flowing tablecloth, Donna's prehensile toes had been groping about in Antonio's lap from *antipasti* to *grappa*.

The meal had been a test for him in more ways than one. Mazzini had been barely able to conceal his fury at the unexpected guest. The land agent had kept telling everyone that Donna had made a mistake and invited Antonio instead of the Contessa Alfere-Tiziano. And he had referred to Antonio as 'our friend the workman' all evening. Antonio did not care. Donna obviously hadn't told Mazzini that she had invited his great rival in the contest for possession of the Palazzo Tiziano, and the thought of Mazzini's annoyance amused Antonio. He smiled to himself. It took one to know one, and in Enrico Mazzini Antonio recognised another man of determination. Mazzini wanted to get his hands on the *palazzo*. It had been obvious from the start of the dinner party that the invitation Donna had been so keen to deliver had been intended only for the Contessa.

No doubt her ladyship would have felt more at home there than I did among the posing, pouting glitterati, Antonio thought. A shadow crossed his features. None of the people he had met at that party knew what it was like to do any real, physical work. He had been able to tell from the pinkly perfect state of their hands. Everything had been handed to them on plates since birth. None of them had really *earned* their living.

Shocked, Antonio found that his hands were clenching into fists as he stared unseeing at the computer screen. Nobody should be in turmoil over such a minor thing, should they? He switched off the machine, but found himself thinking of Rissa again, and the way she had leapt back from his touch. It had worked on him like a bucket of iced water. *If that is the way she wants it, then that is the way it will stay,* he thought bitterly.

Pushing back his chair, he got up to fix himself the first coffee of the day. As he did so, he noticed a rectangle of paper standing out clearly against the dingy industrial carpeting of the site office. It must have been pushed under his door outside of working hours. That was not in itself unusual, as there was no letterbox. Opening the door had pushed the item back, so he had not seen it when entering. Strolling over, Antonio picked up what turned out to be a good-quality envelope, addressed to him. Slitting it open, he saw that it was a list of suggestions for improvement to the *palazzo*, written in neat, well-formed handwriting and signed by the Contessa. She must have delivered it the night before.

What Antonio read in her letter raised his eyebrows as well as his spirits. She wanted to make the estate a commercial paying concern. Antonio was violently opposed to the thought of people traipsing around his property, but he had to admit that her ideas were imaginative. She wanted to involve the local people in decisions made about the future of the house. That showed naïveté—planners and their regulations were the things she had to worry about. The girl might have a fancy title, but it was becoming clear to Antonio that she was not afraid to use either her head or her hands.

Her letter also contained rough plans to develop the many outbuildings as craft workshops, or offices for small businesses. She was even suggesting that one building could be set up as a cyber café. Antonio had doubts about these ideas. Monte Piccolo was not the first call for a holiday destination. The market for dream-catchers, handmade soap or other niche products would be small in summer and probably non-existent in the winter. A computer drop-in centre was only slightly more reasonable, although there was still a problem. People hated going on foot for any distance these days, and the estate building she had earmarked for the project was a good half-mile walk uphill from the village. Visitors would want to come by car, equalling chaos—especially in wet weather. It would also require a lot more additional parking space.

Rissa's third idea made him laugh out loud. She wanted to open an English-style café and plant centre in the grounds of the *palazzo*. Antonio had spent a lot of time in Britain. The food there seemed to be either fried or floury. Sometimes it managed to be both at the same time. He could not see his fellow Italians going for that sort of thing. As for a garden centre—his people were self-reliant and hard-working. If they wanted plants, they took cuttings or sowed seeds. Swapping between neighbours, friends and family was the rule here, rather than the exception. No one would come here to *buy* plants!

The letter's final suggestion wiped the smile from Antonio's face. Rissa had noticed the richness of wildlife in the Piccolo valley, and no one could fail to be impressed by the beauty of the surroundings. The Contessa wanted to turn the grounds of the Palazzo Tiziano into a proper nature reserve. People would be drawn from the towns to experience local wildlife at first hand. There would be observation hides, bird-feeding stations, nest boxes and a whole list of other wildlife-friendly ideas.

This sounded dangerously close to Antonio's own dream of a place close to nature, where he could escape from his hectic life as a billionaire property developer. The estate had already started to work some kind of magic on him in the time that he had been working there. Why shouldn't it do the same for other people? Because this is *my* house, he reminded himself sharply, and I do not intend to have members of the general public wandering about as though they own the place. It is bad enough having to suffer that cuckoo of a Contessa, he thought darkly.

He read the letter again from beginning to end. Despite her grand ideas, there was a hint of uncertainty hiding behind the Contessa's words. She must be desperate for approval. This gave Antonio an illicit thrill of anticipation. Beneath that icy exterior she really must be a nervous little mouse. Why else would she be seeking advice on such major steps from a virtual stranger?

He folded the letter and tapped it thoughtfully against his even white teeth. She might have held out against his temptations so far, but this letter displayed all the signs of a woman in a tight spot. First there had been her idea of selling her clothes. Now she was planning all sorts of schemes. It sounded as though the Contessa needed money, and wanted to use the *palazzo* to help her get it. This was despite the fact that she had no contacts in the village and knew virtually no one. She was reduced to asking him—a man whom her land agent regularly dismissed as nothing more than a workman—for advice. Donna had also warned him that Mazzini was telling the English girl that her site manager was not to be trusted.

Antonio's smile broadened. Any woman who was *this* desperate for support must fall to him eventually. He would be ready to take possession of both her and his birthright when it happened. It might take time, but Antonio had plenty of that. He had the money she clearly lacked, too. The only cloud on his horizon was the growing idea that he might have to let her goad him all the way into marriage. Still, it was a sacrifice he was willing to make. Once he had drawn her in with sex and money, cutting off her supplies of both would soon see the Contessa heading for the divorce courts. When that happened, Antonio would be ready for her. His lawyers were the best in every field, and they would have history on their side. It would be the time when certain cats would be let out of certain bags.

Antonio was looking forward to watching the fall of the house of Alfere, and the idea of a sweet triumph over that beautiful girl gave him still more reason to smile.

His plan could not possibly fail.

CHAPTER SIX

RISSA had been so fired up by her work on the house's exterior that she'd hardly slept that night. After falling into a doze just before dawn, she'd woken with a start. She had been dreaming about footsteps outside her window. Waiting in the half-light, she listened for long moments. All was silent. The thought of being some practical help around the site made her get up, rather than linger too long in bed. Washing and dressing in lukewarm water from the old and criminally unlagged hot water tank, she went downstairs and got busy in the kitchen.

Within a couple of hours the air was rich with the fragrance of baking. Rissa had produced trays full of English teatime treats. When the kitchen door latch clicked, she called out without looking up.

'Oops! Sorry, Livia. I was going to get all this washing up done before you arrived.'

'It isn't Livia. It's me.'

Rissa jumped at Antonio's low, harmonious voice. She whirled around, instantly on her guard, but he had been distracted. Every horizontal surface around the kitchen was lined with the cakes and savouries she had been making, and he was inspecting them minutely.

'I thought I would try out a few things, Antonio…
Although you won't have been to the site office yet this
morning, so you won't know what they are for.'

'On the contrary, Contessa, I was probably in there before
you awoke. I know exactly what all this is about.'

'Oh, really?' Rissa suspected a trap.

'Yes, and I should warn you that your idea is unlikely to
be popular in Italy, where we know how real food tastes. May
I try one of these things you have made?'

He raised an eyebrow, indicating a tiny individual
meringue sandwiched with *crème pâtisserie*. Rissa nodded,
and he put it straight into his mouth.

'This is not English food as I remember it, Contessa,' he
said thoughtfully. 'Your sexual frustration has clearly been
worked through in several useful ways.'

'My *what*?' Stunned, Rissa flapped her teatowel in agitation.

'You know what I mean.' Finishing his cake, Antonio's
fingers hovered between a tray of cheese scones and one of
cherry muffins. 'When we were together the other day, you
got cold feet at the last minute—for whatever reason. It has
left you boiling with energy, which has been looking to find
an outlet. That is why the paintwork at the front of the house
has been so expertly stripped—because you have not got as
far as any other sort of stripping for a while. As for these
cakes—well, it is bound to be some kind of frustrated fertility
rite, don't you think?'

'I resent that!'

'Why? Because it is true?'

'You have got a mighty high opinion of yourself, Signor
Isola. What makes you think I don't have high standards in
every job I attempt?'

'Because I know women.'

'Not this one, you don't.'

'You are going to hand out all this largesse to my work-force, to make them love you even more than they do now.' Antonio had initially chosen a cherry muffin, but as he finished the last morsel he frowned and decided to give in to temptation. Leaning over the cooling trays again, he lifted up a cheese scone.

'I don't need anyone to love me, thank you very much,' Rissa said. But Antonio noticed her expression. He was alert immediately.

'You may not need any mental stimulation, Contessa, but physically you certainly desire it. You wanted me the other day. Confess it.'

'I have no intention of confessing anything, to you or anyone else, Antonio. Now, if you would excuse me, I must get this room cleared up before Livia arrives.'

Draping the teatowel over her shoulder, she turned to put the kettle on to boil for more hot water. She did not hear him go, but some strange instinct told her when he had left the room.

'I don't care what anyone says, *signora*. You are doing a good job here.' Livia said later as she sampled the cakes Rissa had made.

'Are you hinting that somebody is unhappy with my plans?'

Livia gave an uncomfortable smile. 'This place means a great deal to Signor Isola.'

'Yes, but he is only the site manager here. It is going to be *my* home,' Rissa said firmly.

'Only because your husband's family came by the *palazzo* illegally—' The housekeeper stopped as a shadow fell across the kitchen threshold. It was Antonio, returning from the building site.

'I came back to see if you would be available for work today, Contessa.'

His silky words were directed at Rissa, but his eyes were black arrows pinning Livia to her seat.

Rissa took her time in finishing one of the cherry muffins. Licking her fingers with dainty relish, she made him wait for her reply.

'Actually, I wanted to continue cleaning the main reception room—for part of today, at least.' She planned to wipe down the picture frames and dust the canvases of all those supercilious ancestors. That would give Antonio a start. If he thinks his distant forebears had some quarrel with the Alfere-Tiziano family, let him tell them direct to their regal faces, she thought.

'Very well, Contessa.' He started to stroll away, calling back over his shoulder, 'But if you should be at a loose end, come and find me. There are plenty of useful things that you can do.'

Rissa had a few last-minute worries about trying out her cooking on the workmen, but it had to be done. They were exactly the type of people she wanted to attract to the estate. There were plenty of them about, replacing the roof and working on the wiring, so she had a captive audience.

Antonio had strict rules about his men going off-site during working hours. Rissa guessed that his teams of workers might appreciate a break at mid-morning. Their arrogant site manager was so scrupulous about workers' rights that he could hardly complain. The sun was relentless, and the sky was as hard and blue as Lapis Lazuli. It was only proper to offer them all some cake and homemade lemonade in those conditions.

She dressed carefully. Men were men the world over, but Italian men came with a special reputation. Antonio had proved that to her already. She pulled on a soft, stretchy top in pale pink, with long sleeves and a discreet scooped neckline. To play up the demure image, she added a floaty silk skirt and a pair of impractically strappy sandals. These are exactly the type Donna would choose, she thought darkly, then rebuked herself for being catty.

Each working day, Antonio had coffee in his site office at eleven o'clock precisely. It was the time when he attended to paperwork and made urgent phone calls. Rissa knew he would be out of circulation then for an hour or so, and it would give her time to do some market research.

Armed with a tray of delicacies, she set off around the building site. The workmen always looked at her when she passed, but until now it had only been covert glances. Now she was approaching them directly, with something to offer, their expressions were more openly admiring.

'Here you are, gentlemen. This is a little break for you. I'm sure Signor Isola wouldn't deny you a taste of some good old-fashioned English food.'

'Lemonade?' one of them questioned. 'Do they know what real fruit is like in England?' The whole gang laughed at that.

'You would be surprised, *signor*. I have been able to pick some herbs from the *palazzo* gardens for the cheese pastries, and there are fresh wild strawberries in the tarts,' Rissa told them with a smile.

She set down the tray and withdrew a short distance. It was not because she wanted to keep apart from them for social reasons, but because their appreciative expressions were not all directed towards the food. The way they looked at her made her feel uncomfortable.

The men were quick to clear their plates. They had been brought up to love good food that had been freshly prepared, whether it was simple peasant fare or choice local dishes. Soon they were expressing their approval to each other over empty plates and glasses.

Rissa felt a surge of pride. It was another boost to her self-esteem, which had been pretty well squashed from the time she had married Luigi. In his world, women were supposed to do nothing but look beautiful and provide sons. He would have laughed out loud if Rissa had suggested she might be able to make her own living. *But this is what I was born to do*, Rissa thought with sudden realisation. She was relishing the satisfied comments of her customers, and smiled when one of them stacked up the tray with empty crockery and brought it over to where she was standing.

'That was delightful,' he said carefully, in his best English. 'May I carry this back into the house for you, Contessa?'

'Thank you, but I can manage,' Rissa replied with equal politeness. She recognised the look in his eyes and knew it would be safer to distance herself from him, and the faster the better.

'*Si*—yes—but couldn't you find some other use for me…inside, eh?'

He left no doubt about what he meant. Rissa felt sick. Were all men like this, seeing her only in terms of sex? Or was it somehow her fault? Did she give off all the wrong signals?

That was what Luigi had told her. The words he had used on their honeymoon stabbed through her yet again. Over the years she had tried to please him, but nothing had worked. Her love for him had never faltered, but for some reason everything had always been reduced to blame and guilt.

A new nightmare suddenly replaced her old one. The workman was moving in closer to her. She could feel his breath against her skin. Whirling away from him, she stopped dead. Antonio was standing in the open door of the site office.

That is typical of an Englishwoman abroad, he thought fiercely. But the feeling that boiled through his veins was resentment rather than disdain. The sensation annoyed him. Why had she got under his skin in such a way? He strode out into the courtyard, ordering the men back to work.

His instinct was to send Carlo straight down the road without a reference, but that would solve nothing. Not when Rissa herself had behaved in such a manner.

'Get back to work with the others,' he growled at Carlo. The workman shrank beneath Antonio's glare and dissolved into the background. 'Contessa—what does it say about your judgement when you allow things like that to happen?'

Now that Antonio had saved her from the wolf, Rissa managed to rally. Instead of muttering an apology, she faced up to him. 'The men were helping me test the recipes I intend to sell at the café here.'

The girl really did have spirit; there was no doubt about that. *She'll need it*, Antonio thought. And determination too, if she is going to work as hard as I had to.

'How can you be so careless—appearing in public wearing such clothes?'

'What?' Rissa looked at him, mystified. Antonio clicked his tongue.

'That thin skirt is quite transparent in the sunlight. Your legs were the first things I noticed when I appeared at the door of the site office. I dare say that was what stirred up Carlo and the others.'

His words worked better than he had anticipated. With a horrified gasp, Rissa blushed the colour of a Tuscany rose.

'I must go and change!'

'I'll take the tray.' Antonio grasped it as Rissa dashed back into the house. He followed, but not before surveying the work of his staff. He did not want his workmen to think that the sight of Carlo trying to get lucky had aroused anything more than an employer's rage at working time wasted. Antonio chose not to think too hard about what feelings the little scene had really sparked in him.

When he got inside the house, the kitchen was deserted. He could hear Livia, busy upstairs with the new vacuum, so he dumped the refreshment tray on the table and went in search of Rissa.

The door to her suite was closed, and all was silent. Being so close to a pretty girl's bedroom usually triggered an instinct in Antonio to dive in and possess. But after what had happened the last time he had been tempted by her, he was not so sure that those feelings could be trusted. After wrestling with his conscience, he raised his fist and banged on her door.

In one movement Rissa threw it open and bounced out.

'Antonio! What are you doing here?'

Her hands were behind her, and he heard the unmistakable click of a key turning in the lock. That was a pretty clear message. Lifting both hands in a soothing gesture, he took a step back.

'This is not what you might imagine, Contessa. I came to bring you a warning. A friendly note of caution.'

Rissa looked up into his steady dark eyes. There was no trace of fire in them now. Instead they were limpid with concern—*although it makes him even more desirable,* Rissa thought with a pang. *He really is very good-looking...*

'I am concerned only for your welfare, Contessa.'

And charming with it. Rissa felt herself wavering. No man had been so caring towards her for years. It made her appreciate her vulnerability. She wondered, not for the first time, what it would be like to have Antonio's protection surrounding her.

'A woman in your position must take great care of her reputation, Contessa. It reflects upon the dignity of this ancient house.' His gaze travelled appreciatively down the length of her body. 'Thank goodness you have seen sense and changed your skirt. That wisp of silk made you look like a tart,' he finished firmly.

'How dare you?' Rissa gasped, snapping out of her reverie at once. Before she could get into her stride, she was interrupted.

'Cooee—Antonio?' a thin voice trilled. 'The men said you were in here, so I came on up—'

It was Donna. Her tinkling tones advanced up the stairs in the most annoying way.

'This place needs a really good clean,' she said disdainfully. Her nose wrinkled as she inspected her fingertips, which she had just trailed up the banister rail.

'I am so sorry, Donna, but this is a private house. It isn't geared up for visitors.' Rissa smiled sweetly, before turning on her heel and walking off with purpose. She was not about to retreat into her own suite, so she headed for the sound of Livia's vacuuming. Opening the appropriate door, she left Donna and Antonio to their own devices.

Livia switched off the suction as soon as she saw Rissa.

'Ah—you have been speaking with Signor Antonio again.'

'How could you possibly know that, Livia?'

'Oh, because you have roses in your cheeks, *signora*.' The old lady chuckled.

'If I do, it is only because he makes me so angry.'

'He is not so bad. All Antonio needs is a wife to mellow him. A good local girl, to keep him in the valley and feed him up.'

'I don't think a plaster saint could mellow that man.' Rissa sighed. She went over to the dusty window—only to be rewarded by the sight of Antonio squiring Donna to a smart blue cabriolet. One of his hands was patting the small of her back in a gesture that should have been merely polite. Rissa read far more into it.

Good riddance to our unwanted guest, Rissa thought firmly, but something Livia had said triggered an unusual resentment within her. Donna was a local girl. And Antonio had shown himself to be a traditional Italian man. She might not be able to deny his powerful sexual attraction, but his attitude towards her was acting as a great contraceptive.

It isn't as though I have to care what he thinks of me, she thought fiercely. *He doesn't have any finer feelings to offend, and I'm never likely to get entangled with him emotionally.* That image made her pause for a minute, and she had to concentrate hard on the pain he had given her by touching Donna in full view, out there on the terrace. Why did she get such a pang when she saw them together? Was it envy, that they were obviously an item when she was so isolated? Or did the green-eyed monster have something to do with it, too? Rissa was not sure that she wanted to know the answer.

She spent the rest of the day throwing herself into the task of cleaning all the old family portraits. Antonio might be scornful, but she found a strange reassurance from knowing that she was now part of a long line of survivors—even if they were only her relatives by marriage.

It was mid-afternoon before she stood back in the centre of the salon to admire her handiwork. The paintings would need professional restoration as soon as she could afford it, but for the moment a soft duster had worked wonders. One picture of an imposing man on horseback had come up particularly well. She flicked a last speck of dust from his nameplate. Then her heart leapt as she heard a familiar masterful tread on the cobblestones outside. She did not have to look out of the window to know that Antonio was coming into the house.

Rissa had not trusted herself to watch Donna drive away earlier. If Antonio had accepted a lift from the woman then, why was he striding back in here now?

She resented the fact that Antonio spoke so directly to her femininity. Her heart was fluttering and her mouth was dry even before he came into the room. And all this after he had been so critical of her dress sense! When she'd been living in Manhattan, Rissa had heard other wives at the gym say that sex with their staff was the best sort—it was without strings. Then again, they hadn't been involved with Antonio. Those women always held the whip hand with their lovers—sometimes literally. If the guy caused trouble, or began getting above himself, he got the sack. Rissa knew she could never play that card with Antonio. She was relying on him too much.

For most of the time she could almost convince herself that she needed him as her site manager more than she needed his body. When he strode into her salon now, she was not so sure.

'Contessa—you need to come with me and OK the detailed plans for the outbuildings,' he announced sharply.

'I'm surprised you haven't done that yourself,' she said as he held the door open for her to pass through.

'I designed the layout, so you should have at least some say in the final decision.'

'After the way you criticised me this morning, Antonio, I thought you would set more store by your mysterious friend Donna's opinion.' Rissa's cheeks stung again at the memory of their confrontation.

'There is no mystery about Donna—none at all,' he said as they left the main house.

As they rounded a corner Rissa stopped dead. A gleaming red Ferrari Scaglietti crouched outside the site office, as though on guard.

'Good grief! You aren't employing men who can afford something like that, are you?'

'It certainly isn't coming out of your budget, Contessa. She's mine.' Antonio walked forward and ran a hand over the car's bonnet. It was as sleek and shiny as a cherry. Inspecting the scarlet surface, he pulled down the cuff of his shirt and repeated the caress, to remove any traces his naked palm might have left behind.

'You work in construction, yet you drive a car like that?'

'Doing things like *this* allows me to afford trinkets like *that*. You could call it a perk of my profession,' he said, without once taking his eyes off the Ferrari.

Rissa circled this touching love scene to reach the door of his office. 'I'll just check the plans while you two are busy out here, shall I?'

'I shall be there in a second. Then, when we have finished

in the office, I must go into Florence. Would you like a lift? You said a while ago that you were desperate for designer dress shops.'

'That is only because I have a lot of things to sell.' She stared at the gleaming red sportscar. 'There won't be room to pack a single dress box in that thing, let alone transport your building supplies.'

Antonio clicked his tongue. *'That thing!'* he muttered under his breath, then tore himself away from his car to unlock the office for her. 'There is a waiting list for passenger space in my car, Contessa. Though exceptions can always be made…'

'I must sell my dresses to get enough money to pay for all this.' She nodded towards the plans as Antonio indicated where she should sign.

'Then you are serious about getting rid of your things? It is not a joke?' he probed as they left the office again.

'I have never been more serious about anything in my life—except this house. And the two things are one, really. The Palazzo Tiziano needs money, and I don't think I'll ever have enough. What I *do* have are a few beautiful assets.'

Hands on hips, Antonio stood for long minutes savouring some of those assets as she studied his car.

'OK,' he said at length, 'Pack up everything you want to take into town and I shall find transport for it. But first I must put away my car.'

'You can leave it there, if you like.'

Antonio looked at her as though she had suggested exposing a baby.

'You must be joking! She is going straight back under cover.'

'Where do you keep it?'

'In the building that houses the old olive press.'

'I didn't know I had—' Rissa began, and then the penny dropped. 'Ah—the only stone building around here with a lock that actually works! I've never been able to get inside that place.'

'That is because I have the only key.' Antonio patted the pocket of his jeans.

'So—I am supposed to live in a house whose doors can be unfastened with twigs, while your car is locked away safe and secure?'

He looked at her narrowly. 'The Palazzo Tiziano has seen many people come and go, but it has never entertained a Ferrari.' He eased his driver's door open in a heat-haze of testosterone.

Rissa carried on towards the house, pointedly ignoring him as he coaxed the Scaglietti into a graceful arc and drove off in a gentle hiss of gravel.

He arrived back at the main door of the *palazzo* a short time later, this time driving an ordinary white van. Rissa raised her eyebrows as she handed him the first dress box.

'*You'll* be driving a workman's vehicle?'

'Why not? I am a workman.'

Rissa added more shallow boxes to the growing pile in his arms. He stowed them all securely in the back of the van, then returned to open the passenger door for her.

'Wouldn't you rather I drove this thing, Antonio?'

'This is not a time for English driving—or for English speaking, either. We shall speak in Italian all the way to Florence, Contessa. Only when I am convinced you can bargain fluently will I let you do business there alone.'

Obediently Rissa climbed up into the cab, accidentally giving Antonio a good view of her legs. In celebration he crashed through the gearbox as the van buffeted and veered along the *palazzo*'s potholed drive.

Rissa did not have time to question his high-handed attitude. He began firing questions at her in Italian, making her do sums and calculations while he dodged the traffic and sped along the A1. Rissa was glad to reach the edge of the city's pedestrian zone, where Antonio stopped, reversed, and slotted into a tiny parking space in one movement and at a speed that made her queasy.

'What is the matter, Contessa? You have gone pale all of a sudden. If you are worried about haggling in the shops, don't worry. I shall be doing the business for you.'

'Didn't I do well enough on the way here? Livia says my Italian is getting better all the time.'

'You were…' Antonio searched for a word '…adequate, Contessa. But you are not a poker player, that I can tell. I shall do all the talking, and I will make far more money than you ever could. It will be like lifting cherries out of pannetone, believe me.'

'Are you sure?'

He clapped a hand to the van's steering wheel and leaned over to her confidentially.

'Do you think I paid full price for my beautiful car? No.' He grinned and got out of the driver's seat. 'That is why you will let me do all the talking, Contessa.'

Two hours later, Antonio seized Rissa by the elbow and steered her rapidly out of their last appointment.

'Fifty thousand euros!' She gasped as they reached the pavement.

Antonio immediately put a finger to her lips. 'Not in front of the street people, Contessa.'

'That's about…' She calculated frantically, but wasn't up to the task. 'Well, enough to keep the *palazzo* going for a while and pay some back to my aunt and uncle too.'

'You are in debt elsewhere?'

'I owe them, yes.'

'How much?'

'I don't want to talk about it. That's a debt of honour. Surely as an Italian you can understand that?'

Antonio regarded her minutely. Honour was not something he had expected to find in a girl who had married into the Alfere family. He liked to think he was a good judge of character, but it was slowly dawning on him that he might have been too quick in judging her. The suspicion that he might be wrong about something began to grow. Antonio never apologised, because as a rule he never made mistakes. This was unknown territory to him. Clearing his throat, he started off down the street in the direction of the Duomo.

'Let me buy you a drink in celebration, Contessa.'

'Oh, no, I can't let you do that. Not after you've earned me so much money.'

'You haven't got it all in your hands yet,' he warned.

'In which case, let's pick up some bits and pieces and have a picnic on the way home.'

He did not seem impressed, but they walked on for a few more metres before he put his feelings into words.

'Do you know what I could really eat right now? A big, thick bacon sandwich, smothered in tomato ketchup. That is *real* food after a hard day's work.'

Rissa sighed. 'I know how you feel. It's the sort of rubbishy comfort eating that really hits the spot once in a while. What a shame Florence is too sophisticated for that kind of thing.

I can't remember the last time I had one of those,' she finished, with real longing.

'I can,' Antonio said darkly. 'My good friend Ricardo works at the Excelsior. He always keeps a ready supply of ex-pat treats. Some of the English and American visitors there don't like what they call "foreign food".'

'That's tourists for you.' Rissa sighed, feeling very much a tourist herself as Antonio turned away to make a phone call.

Twenty minutes later they were ushered into a suite of rooms that looked like heaven and were perfumed with vases of fresh flowers.

'We can't do this!' Rissa hissed, when Antonio had closed the door behind his heavily tipped friend Ricardo.

'Why not? I happen to know the guy who is staying here very well. He won't mind, and it beats a picnic.'

He lifted a silver lid. It revealed a pile of sliced white bread, overflowing with grilled bacon. Red ketchup had been set out in two white china ramekin dishes complete with silver spoons. There was only one thing missing.

'Oh, no—they haven't brought you any coffee, Antonio.'

'I was in the mood for the full English experience.' He picked up the teapot and filled the two cups that had been provided.

'This is bizarre!' Rissa said as they enjoyed their meal. 'Do you have any other friends in high places, Antonio?'

'I have one or two. Anything Signor Mazzini can do, Contessa, I can do better. You can be sure of that.'

It was such a frank statement that Rissa had to comment. 'You really don't like that man, do you?'

'He does not have the interests of the Palazzo Tiziano at heart, Contessa.'

'And I suppose you do?'

'You should not have to ask that question.'

'No,' she replied, lost in thought. 'Sometimes I think you are more interested in the house and estate than you are in me—I mean, in my wishes,' she corrected herself hurriedly. But Antonio was not about to let the moment pass.

'The Palazzo Tiziano and its estate is part of my family's heritage. As for you…you are an extremely beautiful woman, Contessa. When the dress shop staff were inspecting your dresses, I could not help but wonder what you looked like in each one. Which was your favourite?'

'The full-length black velvet,' she said, without hesitation.

'The strapless one?'

Rissa nodded, as a pearly droplet of butter escaped from her final sandwich and ran down the side of her hand. She put down her bread and started to reach for a paper napkin, but Antonio stopped her. Catching her wrist, he raised it to his lips. Before she knew it, Antonio was tracing the course of the butter with the tip of his tongue.

She immediately snatched her hand away. 'No, don't do that. I don't like it.'

'Yes, you do. You are an extremely sensual woman, Contessa. I could feel it the other day. Making love on the Tiziano grass in the open air may not be your thing—although in my opinion you don't know what you're missing—but there can be no excuses today, Larissa. With the exception of my friend Ricardo, no one in the world knows that we are here.' Taking her hand again, he kissed each finger. All the time he was watching her, watching her with those bitter chocolate eyes.

'I can't,' she pleaded, hoping he could not guess how true that was.

Antonio smiled. 'Of course you can. And you will. It is my wish, Larissa, and your desire.' His voice was a hiss that trickled all the way down her spine.

'No—no, really. It isn't my desire. I don't have any feelings like that. For you,' she added quickly. 'I mean, my husband was the only man that ever—er, well, you know…'

He stopped, suspicious of her motives. 'I know…what?'

'Luigi was my first…' She hesitated, not knowing what to say. *Lover* was not the right word. His frustration and her inexperience had put paid to all that. She had always loved him, right up to the end, but it had never been enough. 'He was my first…partner,' she said eventually.

'But surely you are not saying he was your last? I may have misjudged you in some things, Larissa. And for that I should apologise. However, there is no mistaking the need we have for one another. We want each other. Do not deny it.'

He was speaking about the deep desires that were shaking her body as though they were just another biological process. Rissa could hardly believe she could be so attracted to a man who attached no more importance to her love than Luigi had done. Her husband had seen producing an heir with her as his contribution to continuing the Alfere family line. To Antonio, sex was clearly nothing more than an item ripe for crossing off his 'to do' list. Were all men obsessed only with the end result?

'You are forgetting one important thing, Antonio.' She tried to inject some strength into her voice. 'I don't want you.'

'Look me in the eyes and say that.'

Rissa opened her mouth to deny him again, but there was no time. He leant forward and stole a savage, all-consuming kiss. At that moment all her self-control collapsed. In twenty hot, pounding seconds Rissa became his. She tried to struggle, but when he pulled away his eyes were dark with a fierce desire. She knew it mirrored her own. With a faint primal cry she surrendered, digging her fingers into the sliding muscles of his shoulders as he bent to possess her mouth again. His hands slid down to knead her in the same way he had massaged her naked flesh when she had been lying on the grass. Now she could feel the reaction it caused in him. He was grinding her against a firm ridge that was pushing masterfully against the front of his jeans.

Antonio was exultant. Her instant reaction was perfect proof. She wanted him. In the same way she had needed him to take her on the grass, filling her until the heat of their passion reached meltdown and this desire exploded, blotting out all thoughts of the past.

Reaching for him, she found his erection, straining to be freed from the petty restriction of clothing. In an agony of desire Rissa threw back her head, gasping wordless sounds that told him all he wanted to know. His lips found her throat, his fingers pulled at her shirt. As it fell away he circled her nipple with his thumb, teasing it into a point. Then his mouth followed, moving over her bra. Finally releasing her breast from its confection of silk and lace, he began suckling hungrily like a—

Rissa jerked backwards out of his grasp.

'No. I can't!'

'That isn't what it felt like to me.' Antonio fought to catch his breath. This was not supposed to happen. After that business with the sunbathing, when she had as good as proved herself already spoken for, he had intended to keep things light. The trouble was, the nearness of her always had such an effect on him. One touch was all it took to blow away his best intentions and sacrifice his self-control.

'This is not a good idea, Antonio,' she said shakily.

'Of course it is,' he snapped. 'We want each other, and this is the perfect opportunity.'

'That is why it is wrong. I should never have agreed to be alone here with you.'

Frustrated and confused, Antonio had no option but to release her. They had been so hot for each other. What had happened to change it?

The question tormented him all through their painfully silent drive home. Only one thing was certain in his mind. Antonio had never been defeated by a challenge before, and this damned well wasn't going to be a first. He was going to have the Contessa Larissa Alfere, however long it took.

He could wait.

CHAPTER SEVEN

RISSA tried to avoid Antonio altogether after that, but it was impossible. Next day he approached her in the garden, on the pretext of bringing a drink from Livia.

'You said that you owe your parents money, Contessa?'

Rissa put down her tools and brushed off her hands. She had been helping to rake out the stones of the *palazzo*'s structure, ready for the workmen to start repointing. It was a dirty, boring job, but it needed to be done. Rissa reasoned that if it was something she could manage, it freed up a member of Antonio's skilled team to do more valuable work.

She bit her lip, gazing out across the countryside. Her excitement at selling those dresses should not have goaded her into letting that little detail slip.

'I went too far, Antonio. I said something I now regret.'

'It aroused my suspicions. I have seen too much of life to believe the best in people. You must either be very duty bound or very guilty to still be supporting your parents at your age. Which is it?'

'It isn't either of those things. I simply owe them a great deal.' She bent over to dust down the knees of her jeans. It should have told him she was unwilling to continue the conversation, but as she straightened Antonio handed her a glass of lemonade. That killed any hope of escaping into the house. He had stopped her from using the need to fetch a drink as an excuse.

'You have borrowed a lot of money from your parents?' That idea had caught his attention.

'N-no. That's wrong on both counts. They are not my parents; I'm adopted. They have been so generous over the years, because I was everything to them. Now it is time to pay them back.' She took a long drink to hide her discomfort.

'Ah. Then it *is* guilt that drives you?'

'No, not at all!' She reddened and looked away.

Antonio felt as though he had been cheated. Why wouldn't she open up to him? Women were usually only too anxious to talk, trying to ensnare him in their plans. Why was this one so different? More importantly, why did he find himself so bothered about her evasiveness? Because I am concerned at having such a secretive person living in my ancestral home, he told himself. It is nothing more than that. His mind kept on working at the problem as she sipped her drink and tried to ignore him. Antonio did not know which annoyed him more.

'Ah…I know what it is, Contessa,' he said at last. 'You went all out to make an advantageous marriage to a spectacularly wealthy man so that you could siphon off his money in their direction to assuage your guilt—'

'Certainly not!' she flared with annoyance.

Antonio was a seasoned interviewer. He knew that silence was often a more successful tool than interrogation. Sure enough, as he waited, Rissa could not stand his continued scrutiny.

'Luigi had more to worry about than my parents. I tried my best never to trouble him with their concerns,' she recalled sadly.

Antonio congratulated himself. He had succeeded in

business because he was a shrewd judge of character. He knew when somebody was putting up a barrier, and he was as skilled at demolishing defences as he was in building houses. Larissa Alfere might give the impression of a marsh-mallow, but she had constructed a solid centre to protect something deep within her. He was determined to chip away at it to reach the kernel of her truth.

'You were ashamed of the poverty of your upbringing and tried to keep the two halves of your life hidden from one another?'

'How dare you?'

Antonio raised his hands. 'It is something to which I can relate—believe me, Contessa. I did not mean to offend you.'

She had bridled at his explanation, and he expected her to either storm off or change the subject. She did neither.

'Since you seem determined to find out the truth, Antonio, my husband was a proud man who despised need or weakness in others. He expected everyone to be a winner. That is why it hit him so hard when there were parts of his life that were…not so successful. He had enough to worry about, without me pestering him. I had to develop my own methods for helping Aunt Jane and Uncle George.'

'You poor little thing!' Antonio mocked, but stopped when she levelled a fiery glare at him.

'You cannot imagine how hard it is to know that the people you love are suffering.'

'I do know,' he murmured, but Rissa was still burning with the memory of it all.

'I was so desperate to help them I had to become devious. I persuaded Luigi that some of my expenses had to be paid in cash. You know how popular the black economy is. People like hairdressers, florists and personal trainers often prefer to be paid off the books, rather than by cheque or direct debit. It is a regular thing in the City.'

'And among builders,' he said tersely, recalling their earlier conversation.

'I always did things properly. But because I'd heard other women talking about what they got up to, I knew how money could be found to help my aunt and uncle. By saving up small amounts of cash at a time there would be no paper trail, and Luigi would not trace what I was doing with his—I mean, my money.'

Antonio gave a silent whistle. 'How long did you manage to keep it up?'

'My husband never found out.' Rissa shook her head slowly, remembering how terrible it had made her feel. 'He enjoyed the idea of working the black economy by giving me cash. Nothing infuriated him more than paying tax, so he loved to think that the Revenue was losing out.'

'Didn't he notice that you were cutting corners?'

Rissa gave a brittle laugh. 'No one needs their hair done every day, or their flower arrangements replaced according to each change of outfit. As for the Filipino body-shaper—one whole floor of our Manhattan apartment block was given over to gym equipment and pools. I was quite capable of exercising on my own. Walking around town and using the subway saved money, and kept me fit, too.'

Antonio's brow creased in a frown. 'I have never known a woman who would willingly give up any of the advantages she could extract from a man.'

'You've obviously been hanging around with the wrong sort of girl,' Rissa said casually, thinking of Donna. 'I managed well enough—although if I had known the sort of debts Luigi was going to leave I would have squirrelled away a lot more money to cover them.'

'Are all Manhattan wives engaged in this type of racket?'

'I have no idea. I didn't exactly fit into their set, so they were never keen on sharing anything more than idle pleasantries with me. Everything I learned came from accidentally overhearing their chatter. Some of them have extremely loud voices.'

Antonio was miles away, thinking of her free-flowing auburn hair rippling in the breeze as she jogged through Central Park.

'They snubbed you?'

She lowered her lashes and avoided looking at him. 'It didn't matter. I have always been a bit of a loner.'

Antonio felt a surge of distaste at the thought of what she must have endured. He had seen the lifted and Botoxed features of rich women harden still further when one of their circle did anything out of the ordinary. Their jealousy must have been poisonous when they'd been faced with this natural little beauty, he thought with a pang of protectiveness. How could anyone treat her like that?

'Is that why you were happy to come to the Palazzo Tiziano?'

Rissa took another long, slow drink of lemonade. Then she handed him the glass, with her thanks. Realising that he was not going to learn any more, Antonio watched her turn back to the unforgiving stones and set to work again.

Rissa tried to hide her pain by bending over the task in hand. Antonio had stirred so many agonising memories within her. Her first meeting with Luigi had swept her away on a tide of adoration. Money had been the last thing on her mind then. Obviously the fact that Luigi dressed so well had struck her from the moment their eyes had met across the diner, but it had never been an issue between them. A far darker spectre had come to haunt their relationship.

Things had come to a head when he had travelled with her to inner-city London and visited her adoptive parents at home. Luigi had been polite, but distant for the whole afternoon. Rissa had accepted that, as the Silverdale family's circumstances were so different from his own. But the explosion had come as they'd been talked through the fourth album of Rissa's baby pictures. Luigi had stormed out of the house. Rissa had followed him, frantic, and from that moment their relationship had changed. There had been no need to pretend any more.

The one thing that the whole of their world had been waiting for, from the old Contessa to all the occupants of the Keir Hardy Buildings, was not going to happen. It was a release for Rissa, but not her husband. His pride and the weight of family expectation had crushed the life from him. The man Rissa had loved had begun to disappear behind a haze of cigarette smoke and alcohol fumes. She'd persuaded him to seek help, hoping the setback would be temporary, but Luigi had been too immersed in his own unhappiness.

Despite their troubles, Rissa had never stopped loving him. The suspicion that it was her fault had always shadowed the back of her mind. Perhaps she had not been attractive enough, or eager enough. Sex had never been spoken about at home while she was growing up. She had been an innocent when she'd married Luigi, and had learned little from him. All Rissa knew about sex had been picked up from gossip around the gym, so she had had no answers to their problems. She had convinced herself she must be frigid, but the way her body and mind reacted to Antonio was now making her wonder. She wanted him, but she was scared. If at the last moment something went wrong, he would discover what Luigi must have known all along—that she could not please a man. Despite the turbulence of her need, Rissa could not bear to lay herself open to such heartache again.

She was so wrapped up in herself that she scratched her probe blindly between the stones, lost in thought. She had known nothing but love and care from her adoptive parents. To deny them the grandchild they craved had been an added cruelty. They would have doted on a baby. Rissa wondered wistfully if she would ever be lucky enough to give them what they wanted. This was a hard, cruel world in which to bring up a child.

They said that when poverty came through the door love went out of the window, but money brought its problems, too. Rissa was being careful with the windfall her dress sale had brought, and was keeping an even closer eye than usual on the *palazzo* project's cash flow. This had led her to become suspicious of Mazzini, her land agent. One of Antonio's suppliers had written to her directly, asking why a payment of ten thousand euros had been blocked by order of Enrico Mazzini. Rissa had tried ringing her agent's office, but had been told he would not be in until that afternoon. Uneasily, Rissa had made arrangements to pay the supplier direct. Antonio had confirmed to her that the order had been delivered, on time and in full, so there had been no alternative.

Her spirits were sinking with doubt. Mazzini was always so dismissive of Antonio and his advice. Yet the workmen and supplies that Mazzini recommended were far more expensive than those used by Antonio. She had discovered in a round-about way that Mazzini's friends and relatives controlled several of the dearer suppliers. Rissa might not know much about the building trade, but cronyism did not seem a good reason for her to be spending more money.

Antonio could tell she was troubled. He'd touched a raw nerve. The way she had suddenly shut down suggested it. The Alfere marriage might not have been as perfect as the glossy magazines always said, he thought wryly.

He felt moved to reach out to her, to salve whatever wounds that toad Alfere might have inflicted. Then he brought himself up short. That was in the past—a distant time unknown to him. She was a grown woman now, and one that he fully intended to have.

'I can't concentrate on this with you standing over me like a thundercloud, Antonio. I'm going inside to try and contact Signor Mazzini again.'

'Larissa!'

His tone made her drop her hand-fork in shock. She blinked up at him.

'I know that events in the hotel inflamed you as much as they affected me.'

Colour began to creep up from her breasts to her face.

'That is not something I wish to rekindle, Antonio. I should never have agreed to go into that suite alone with you. It was…an oversight.' She could not look at him directly. He could feel the tension preparing her body for flight, and eased his tone.

'Don't forget that for a few precious moments, Contessa, we enjoyed ourselves. There was clearly something happening between us. As a red-blooded male, it is not a feeling I am willing to deny. Where would be the harm in it?' His voice was low and caressing now. 'We are both free agents. As sensible adults there can be no recriminations when neither of us have any strings or commitments.'

No commitments. The words fizzed through Rissa's already overheated mind. She knew he had a point. What would it matter? A pulse began to drum in her ears. It was true that she had vowed never to become emotionally entangled with a man again. And Luigi and Antonio were so similar in some ways, with their direct masculinity. She was wary of giving her heart, only to see it trampled again. On the other hand, if there was no danger of important feelings being involved…

Other women did it. She had heard them in the hairdressers or the gym, discussing their latest sexual adventures. Satisfying their baser instincts never seemed to worry them. On the contrary, casual sex without any messy, emotional baggage was often the only thing that kept those sad, meaningless women functioning.

'Love is one complication that I don't need in my life at the moment,' she announced briskly. There could be no honey without the comeback of a thousand bee stings—she had learned that from her life with Luigi.

Antonio shrugged. 'Who needs love? I am talking about sex, Contessa—not so pure, but simple. You want me, Larissa. Admit it.'

Rissa had to make two attempts before the word emerged. 'Perhaps.'

He chuckled. It was a deep, provocative sound.

'I knew you would agree eventually.'

'I suppose a man like you can spot all the signs?'

'Experience counts for a great deal,' he allowed. 'Although I pick and choose my conquests with care. Are you as choosy, Contessa?'

The question stung her, and she jumped as though it was a physical shock.

'I—I think I should still be in official mourning for the Count. That is not the sort of question you should be asking me.'

'But it *will* be OK for me to take you to bed?' Antonio supplied evenly.

Rissa twisted her hands together. There was so much that was alien and scary about all this, but Antonio had been such a help and support to her. He had worked out what needed to be done around the *palazzo*, hired the workforce, and was pushing ahead with the restoration at speed. The class divide meant nothing to her—after all, she was probably from lower stock than he was—but the gossip columns would go into overdrive if they got hold of a 'Contessa and her site manager' story.

'A woman in my position has to be extremely careful, Antonio.'

'You are thinking of "Kiss and Sell"?' His eyes were checking out all those places he burned to touch, but his mind was clear. They might kiss, but the only one selling anything would be her. And it would be the Palazzo Tiziano that would be changing hands, not money.

'It's no good wasting time talking like this, Antonio. I—I really must go and arrange a meeting with Signor Mazzini.'

His eyes ignited at the mention of the other man's name, and the expression in them almost melted the last of Rissa's reservations.

'Why? I have everything under perfect control here.'

'Yes, but I need to make sure things keep on running as smoothly as they have been doing so far.'

'This would not be an excuse to escape from me, would it?'

'What on earth do you mean?'

'It isn't an attempt to preserve your dignity? Are you afraid I might be about to take you here and now?'

Rissa knew it was time to put her foot down.

'No. It is merely the fact that daytime is for working, while the night—' She faltered.

'Oh, you are surely not going to allow yourself to be tied down to that boring old tradition, are you, Contessa? If you want me, it cannot be constrained by some socially acceptable timetable.'

'What are you suggesting, Antonio? You won't take any wages—' She gave him a wary look and he picked up on it.

'That is true. And I have no need to become your male prostitute. Unless the thought appeals to you, of course,' he finished smoothly.

Despite his casual reply, Rissa realised he had been stung by any suggestion that he would want to be paid for the privilege. Clearly he enjoyed coming on like a wolf, and wanted to be in control.

'It doesn't,' she said quickly.

'You don't need to be so defensive, my lady. Plenty of women enjoy the chance to do a little dominating.'

His voice was arousing her, caressing each word before he let it fall into her breathless silence. She longed to submit to his seductive technique, to the powerful play of those muscles beneath the smooth warmth of his skin, the fragrance of his masculinity and the power of his personality...

Rissa felt a tremor ripple through the very core of her femininity and gasped aloud. She was lost.

'This time it would be for you, Contessa. You can—' Antonio stopped, sensing that someone was approaching. One of the roofing contractors was heading in their direction for a consultation.

Antonio stepped away from her to sort the matter out,

giving Rissa time to catch her breath. Her whole body was on fire. His words alone could make her respond like this, and she shivered at the thought of what might lie in store for her.

'The men will be finishing for the day in about half an hour. That gives you time to go and deal with Signor Mazzini.'

Rissa nodded. She could not speak. Antonio had brushed every sensible thought from her head. He had played on her sensitivities and she felt stripped naked beneath his acquisitive eyes. She had revealed more to him in these few days than she had to anyone else. Now her emotions were quivering with—what? Was it apprehension—or might it even be excitement? She could hardly dare to admit it. At least satisfying her desperate need for him would get this madness out of both their systems.

Antonio watched her pick up her hand-fork again and walk back into the house. Not for the first time she had surprised him. He had expected this to be a simple, bloodless matter of convincing a woman she would give him anything he wanted. He had had no problems achieving this aim in the past. But this was different. No woman had made him hunger as Larissa Alfere did. No other woman had shown such potential to catch fire beneath his hands. It had trembled through her, from that river of russet hair right down through those long, long legs. He savoured that picture of her and—

Rissa could feel him watching her, and had to make a determined effort to stride rather than scuttle back into the *palazzo*. As soon as she had learned the rules of love according to Luigi, she had encased herself in a protective shell. Antonio had been working away at her until she was powerless to resist. How had he managed it? More importantly, what would happen now?

* * *

Livia already had their meal waiting on the kitchen table. Rissa had taken her place and was cutting into her courgette bruschetta before Antonio strolled in. Eating his meals in the kitchen was one of Antonio's few concessions to being in charge.

'Ah—Signor Antonio—someone called Marian rang you, from Cardiff.'

'Cardiff?' Rissa said, with a quick look at Antonio.

'Yes—that is what I said.' Livia fussed in the pocket of her apron. Pulling out a crumpled piece of paper, she smoothed out the creases and read it carefully.

'She says that as you were in charge of providing the new hospital wing, it is only right that you are the one who opens it. She would like to know if you would be free for their official ceremony on the twenty-seventh? Apparently your personal number has been unobtainable recently.'

He did not look pleased. Sitting down at the table, he helped himself to some cold roasted peppers.

'It sounds as though you will have to manage without me for a few days, Contessa.'

'You don't sound very keen.'

'Unlike the great and good of London and New York, I hate publicity.'

'Perhaps if you check your schedule, you could find an excuse not to go?' Rissa frowned. The huge wall chart over in the temporary building was covered with his careful script and various colour-coded labels. It had the status of a holy relic among his workforce.

'Everything stops for Marian,' he said succinctly, pouring out glasses of iced mineral water for all three of them.

Rissa wondered what he meant. The adoring look Livia was giving the unsuspecting Antonio made her think that this

Marian might have let the housekeeper into more secrets than she was revealing.

'Is it all right if I leave early today to take Fabio to the vet, Contessa? Signor Antonio said it would be OK, but I wanted to check with you first.'

I'm sure he did, Rissa thought, brought back to reality. It was hopeless to try and remember if Antonio had mentioned anything to her about the matter. He had bewitched her completely with all his talk of pleasure. Rissa could not even recall if they had really arranged an assignation—whether he had put the words into her mind, or if he had suggested it aloud.

'Of course, Livia,' Rissa said, without looking up from her meal. It was on the tip of her tongue to tell the housekeeper not to bother with the washing up, but any hint that she might be keen to get Livia out of the way would only give Antonio the impression that she was desperate for him. *But then, isn't that the case?* Rissa thought as Antonio suddenly pushed aside his meal and stood up.

'If you are ready to go now, Livia, I will walk you down to the village. I'm sure it won't hurt the Contessa to do her own washing up for once.'

'Oh, but *signora—signor*—I would not want to put you to any trouble!' Livia said, already taking off her apron and flipping it into the washing machine.

'There's no problem. I need the exercise.' Without looking at Rissa, he swung away from the table and held the kitchen door open for Livia.

Rissa's appetite evaporated instantly. She had been keyed-up for him to make another move on her as soon as Livia disappeared. Now her passion was reaching fever-pitch, he had gone.

CHAPTER EIGHT

For the first time since moving in on the estate, Antonio began making a point of avoiding Rissa. After all his taunts about the way she kept getting cold feet, he was now beginning to wonder whether sex with her—emotionless or otherwise—was such a good idea. The more he learned about her, the more he realised this was not going to be a simple conquest.

He concentrated on his work, moving between the various groups of builders with ease. This meant he was always busy.

Rissa tried to convince herself she was glad he now distanced himself from her. He was always tied up, discussing things or talking on the telephone.

She had caught enough snippets of his conversations over the weeks to know that he had several other building projects in progress, both in Italy and Great Britain. She had misjudged him. He was no rootless part-timer, but a true businessman, with fingers in plenty of pies. There were lots of calls on him, and she was becoming increasingly curious about his private life. When Antonio had left to attend the hospital opening in Wales, Rissa had wondered if he travelled there with company. She hadn't seen Donna from the time he'd left until the day he returned.

Mazzini had certainly acted as though he was a free agent while Antonio was away. Rissa had had to refuse invitations from him on an almost daily basis. Her fingers had been burned early on, when, in her naïveté, she had accepted a formal invitation to take a working lunch in Florence. Rissa had been too nervous to eat much. She had stuck to a simple salad and mineral water, despite Mazzini's encouragement. That had been just as well, for she'd discovered later that Mazzini's own generous helpings had been charged to her account with the land agency. It had been a harsh lesson, and Rissa had been wary of mixing business with pleasure ever since.

Her attitude had done nothing to dampen Mazzini's enthusiasm, and he'd called into the *palazzo* every afternoon in Antonio's absence. Rissa had made it clear that she did not expect all these visits to show up on the accounts. Mazzini had claimed to be hurt at the very suggestion, spreading his plump pink hands wide in a gesture of innocence. His smile had almost convinced Rissa, but she was still cautious. She was keeping a close eye on her finances. She had separated her own private funds from the *palazzo* accounts, and knew exactly how much she could afford to spend. An extravagant agent was not an allowable expense. She had enough of those already.

Antonio's trip to Cardiff had been a success, although it did not feel like it. He'd called into the offices of AMI Holdings. They were missing him, but everything was humming along almost as usual. Attending the hospital open day, he'd accepted praise from the staff whose new wing bore his name, but it had not been enough. Something was missing from his life.

He started for home, still trying to pin the feeling down. As he crested the last hill above the *palazzo*, he felt sure that his first sight of home would fill the void. It didn't. He continued his journey hopefully, but still felt faintly cheated as he nosed his Ferrari into a parking space directly outside the house. Getting out of the car he gazed around, uncertain what he was looking for. Suddenly a movement made him look up. Rissa was standing at a window, waving to him. He waved back, and then went straight up the steps into the house.

Abandoned on the gravel, his Scaglietti waited patiently for him to remember that he had left her unlocked.

The guest suite was nearly finished. Rissa could hardly contain her excitement, as it meant her step-parents would soon be able to come and live with her. They had ventured out of England only once before, to attend Rissa's wedding, and she was determined this trip would be even better. She had learned from Antonio. Failing to plan meant you were planning to fail, he always said. So she telephoned one of Luigi's old friends. He lived in London, and was the editor of an upmarket lifestyle magazine. The offer of an exclusive photo-shoot when the *palazzo* was complete proved to be irresistible. He agreed to accompany the Silverdales on their forthcoming journey to Monte Piccolo.

Privately, Rissa wondered how much the chance to make up to a supposedly rich widow had persuaded him. Luigi had always been insanely jealous of the man's interest in her, although the Count had managed to hide his envy at the time. Freddie Tyler was far too influential to be upset, and now Rissa intended to use that influence for her own ends.

When Freddie saw the potential contained in her beautiful home, he would be sure to give it a good write-up. Publicity should attract holidaymakers to the area, which was already trying to publicise itself now that locals could take pride in 'their' *palazzo*, and visitors would help the economy of Monte Piccolo, as well as Rissa's finances. The gardens were producing well, and she had designed a website to advertise everything. Her early training in marketing had taught her to be ready to take advantage when and where she could. Lucky breaks came to those who planned ahead.

As the date of completion drew nearer, Livia decided to get into character. She bought herself some severe black dresses, and took to wearing a collection of keys at her waist like a dignified châtelaine.

'I shall need a full list of Mr and Mrs Silverdale's likes and dislikes, *signora*, together with those of Mr Tyler, well in advance of their arrival,' the housekeeper announced in her new ultra-efficient manner.

'Of course, Livia. But you don't need to make any distinction between them. Every guest is going to be treated like royalty here. I shall just be so glad to see some friendly faces—besides yours, of course,' she added with a smile. Livia had thawed out quickly once she had realised that Rissa was not brain-dead, like most of the women who had been attracted to the Alfere family in the past.

In her original list of suggestions for Antonio, Rissa had said she wanted to produce as much food at the *palazzo* as possible. To her surprise, mountains had been moved and miracles had been worked. It had happened. Antonio had mobilised his troops. They had spent one precious afternoon of perfect weather clearing, levelling and grading an area where Rissa could make a garden. She had added seeds and water, which had sprung into life as if by magic. And, one morning each week, Livia had been taking grapes, lemons, salad bunches and other vegetables down to sell at the market. The money only trickled in, but the effect it was having on Rissa's self-confidence was out of all proportion to the small amount of cash the estate was earning. She could look forward to having her own money again.

A few euros spent at the market on plants and seeds had produced an almost instant effect. The reverse had happened with the *palazzo*. Rissa had poured money in, and things had looked more and more desperate. Now, all of a sudden, the house blossomed. With the *palazzo* structurally sound, and part of the garden a thing to be proud of rather than a wilderness, Rissa decided to throw a party for the locals. The people in the village were her future customers, and her enterprise could only grow with their help. She had heard from Livia that the people of Monte Piccolo were curious to know exactly what was going on inside 'the big house'. Some of them had even been peering in through gaps in the stonework of the estate wall when they thought no one was looking. Now was a good time for her to hold an open house. It would keep people interested, and with luck it would give them something to look forward to.

Entertaining at home was an exciting new idea for Rissa. Her step-parents never invited people to their house because they were ashamed of their relative poverty. Luigi had always hated having people in any of his homes. He'd preferred it to be just the two of them—and the old Contessa.

Rissa could not wait to fill her new house with sound and laughter. It was empty and echoing at the moment. With no soft furnishings or carpets in place yet, it seemed the ideal opportunity for welcoming anyone who wanted to come. There was also another reason for her generosity. Since arriving at the *palazzo*, Rissa had spent most of her time wearing old clothes. She was either working in the garden or sorting through abandoned rooms. Before Luigi's death she had felt faintly embarrassed by the designer clothes he bought for her at every opportunity. Now, for once, she could not wait for an opportunity to dress up again.

Slipping away to the room where the last of her expensive clothes were stored, Rissa spent some time marvelling at the remnants of the extravagant lifestyle that had once been hers. Beautiful gowns, bias-cut to show off her slender figure, reminded her of dinner parties that had continued until daybreak. There were elegant suits for attending the races in Kentucky, tea dresses worn to Washington receptions, and silken peignoirs designed for wearing at home when doing not very much at all. Hers had been a life of privilege and inertia. Compared to the hard work and worry of her time at the *palazzo*, Rissa now realised she had been living a half-life until arriving in Italy. She had been vegetating, when she might have been experiencing real life. Despite everything, this was *fun*.

Her party was planned to coincide with the afternoon's *passeggiata*. Rissa hoped that people would follow the signs set up at the estate gates, leading them through to the grounds beyond. Their curiosity would be rewarded on the terrace in front of the house. Rissa had borrowed some tables and covered them with lace curtaining rescued from inside. These had washed up a treat, and been bleached by the sun. There was lemonade made with the estate's own fruit, wine from a local supplier, and free samples of the type of food she was hoping to sell in the *palazzo* café.

When all the arrangements were well under way, Rissa

showered and changed. It was a novelty to have water spraying from the showerhead in her new luxury bathroom rather than from some accidental leak about the place. She spent a long time luxuriating, but luckily it never took her long to get ready. A touch of lipstick and a suspicion of face powder was enough, given the healthy glow that outdoor living was giving her.

She had already chosen what she would wear: a white linen skirt, teamed with a sleeveless navy top sprinkled with polka dots. It was too hot for the matching jacket, so she left that behind on its hanger. Scooping her thick, dark hair into a clip, she added a thin gold bracelet and matching necklace. Then she spritzed on the last of her Chanel, and went out to meet her public.

The building team had already gathered, almost unrecognisable in shirts and trousers. They usually strolled about in shorts, stripped to the waist. Now they stood about in uncomfortable groups. Antonio was the only one who looked at ease. He was wearing a light-coloured linen suit, teamed with a cotton shirt open at the neck, giving a hint of body hair. This illicit glimpse of his smooth brown skin aroused Rissa more than his fully bare chest might have done. It was the allure of the half-hidden, and she had to fight the temptation to feast her eyes on him openly.

It worried her that in five years of marriage Luigi had never been able to ignite half the feelings within her that she could get from simply looking at Antonio. Merely to walk past him made her pulse pound, and she found herself inhaling deeply so that she could catch the clean, male scent of him.

She was scared. Her body was reacting in ways she had never known before. It was taut with expectation today. Parties were when things happened, weren't they? What if Antonio took her aside and tempted her again? With one murmured request he could undo her resolve not to give in—that was all it would take. If he wanted her then she was his. No question. There would be no denying him this time. Her body was seeing to that.

And who was Rissa to deny herself? She had been a good, loyal wife, despite all her troubles. That torture had ended with Luigi's death. Now she was free, why shouldn't she indulge herself for once?

Anticipation added a champagne fizz of excitement to her already heightened senses. There were so many questions still whirling around in her head. If she slept with Antonio, would she hate herself for giving in to temptation, or look on it as one of life's great experiences? Perhaps once would not be enough? Glancing at him covertly, Rissa knew it would not. She had given her heart once and seen it battered. Could she bear to go through that again?

But she might be running ahead of herself. Surely Antonio Isola could have any woman he wanted? The look in Donna's eyes each time they met made that clear enough. His drive and ambition on behalf of the Palazzo Tiziano must surely be mirrored in his intimate life. He was all male, and would take every opportunity to prove it. If he wanted to bed Rissa, surely he would have thrust aside her doubts and taken advantage of her before now?

The thought of his touch on her body brought a fierce glow, but it was a pleasure that might never be tasted.

Rissa moved through her guests in a dream. She smiled her thanks at their appreciation and exchanged a few words here and there. All the time she kept her face turned away from where she knew Antonio to be. She was scared he could read her thoughts, and she knew her eyes would betray her innermost feelings. She did not want his probing intelligence working out how vulnerable she felt in the face of his charm. When all was said and done, the careful weighing up of advantages and disadvantages counted for nothing when matched against her raw, pulsating need for him. One word, one look from him, and Rissa knew she would be in his arms and in his bed, making all her fantasies reality.

Antonio paced around the party like a caged lion. He was restless with desire, and resented it. The Contessa Larissa Alfere-Tiziano was supposed to have been a minor diversion on the road to acquiring his *palazzo*, but something had happened. Somewhere along the line, simple physical desire for her had been overtaken by a real need. Antonio knew all about satisfying plain, old-fashioned lust. That was a game for the flippant and shallow. What he was experiencing now craved a deeper satisfaction, an eternal pleasure. His body ached with it.

Seeing Rissa drifting through her flocks of admirers, seemingly oblivious to the effect she was having on them, seized his insides and screwed them up. The women watched her easy, understated elegance and style. The men appreciated that too, but in less subtle ways. Rissa seemed to rise above it all, treating the appreciative looks with a gentle innocence.

He wondered what the audience would do if he gave in to temptation and grabbed her right now. He would kiss her until that coolly aristocratic body melted in his arms and responded with the hot passion he had kindled in her before and could not wait to taste again.

* * *

The entertainment was not all one-way. Although the locals had come to inspect their new neighbour, and see what she was doing to the old place, Rissa was learning too. Elderly people—some of whom had worked at the *palazzo* in the old days—were keen to share their memories. Mothers, grateful for somewhere new to push their buggies, fed grapes and lemonade to toddlers in the shade of the fig trees. Middle-aged couples came to poke around the gardens. But Rissa was disappointed that there were no youngsters at her party.

There were plenty of them hanging around street corners, in their counterfeit fashions and designer sunglasses, but the way young people were being priced out of Monte Piccolo was not their only problem. Teenagers who stayed in the area had nothing to do. And kids with time on their hands could lead to trouble. Rissa began to wonder about expansion plans even before her ideas for the *palazzo* were up and running. Perhaps Antonio would reconsider having one of the out-buildings made into a cyber café? He had already talked her into having the main house wired for multimedia and communications. She could not imagine that it would cost much more to run cables through to another building.

She risked glancing in his direction, and stiffened. Donna had appeared, and was talking to him with animated delight. Antonio smiled at her physical nudges, but glanced away often, to study the depths of his half-full glass of Chianti. What are they talking about? Rissa wondered as Donna lifted a ripe fig from one of the wicker fruit baskets set along the length of the tables. As the woman took a bite, rich juice spilled down her chin, making her laugh. It tickled Antonio's fancy, too, and as he joined in Donna raised her fruit to his laughing lips, kissing them with the sweet, unctuous flesh.

Savage, aching jealousy suddenly gripped Rissa. Burning, she turned away. *I must have been mad to think of trying to talk business with Antonio at a time like this,* she thought. *He is too busy making up to that—that woman.*

Rissa busied herself topping up the glasses of her many guests. Livia had been forbidden to wear her uniform, and was under instructions just to mingle and enjoy herself. When Rissa went looking for her housekeeper, she found her seated beneath a great spreading holm oak with a covey of other matrons. They were busy sizing up the guests.

'Thank the good Lord those builders came wearing clothes!' Livia announced as Rissa offered them all more *biscotti*. Her friends clucked indignantly.

'It is not right that a *contessa* should be subject to such sights—with the exception of one young man, maybe.' Someone in the coven chuckled. They were all looking at Rissa with such mischievous delight that she was immediately suspicious.

'What do you mean by that, ladies?'

'You must know, *signora*,' Livia explained. 'It has been a long time since a true Michaeli-Tiziano lived in this house. Make sure the place is not much older before the family line is secured, Contessa.'

Rissa looked at her housekeeper quizzically.

'Find yourself a nice young man and fill the place with *bambini* as quick as you can, Contessa.' A hook-nosed harridan wagged a finger at her. 'The old names must continue.'

'She *has* a nice young man. And not only that, he is a—'

'Livia! Is there any more wine?' Antonio's voice cut

through Rissa's astonished silence. He was bearing down on the group beneath the tree like a thundercloud.

'This is Livia's day off. Perhaps I could get you some?' Rissa said sweetly as the old ladies nudged each other and murmured together. They smiled, realising that Rissa was looking back at them. She could not help but think that there was something sinister about their talk—and Antonio's oh-so-convenient interruption.

'It isn't for me,' he said sharply. 'The general supply is running low.'

Rissa did not wait to see if Livia's friends would explain what they meant. She was more concerned to make sure her party was running smoothly.

'Ah, Antonio!' Donna arrived at his side again, to attach herself to his arm. 'Enrico keeps warning me that you are un-trustworthy, but I guess I just like playing with fire.'

'Excuse me, Donna. I must circulate.'

The dark-eyed beauty flashed a savage look at Antonio as he interrupted her flirtation once again by striding off through the crowds. Her resentment turned to anger as she saw that he was threading his way through the guests with a purpose. He was heading to where Rissa stood, as dignified as any of the Tiziano family portraits.

Dusk was creeping up from the east, and Rissa was wondering how to wind things up tactfully. It had been a good party, and most people had already drifted away—but not Donna. Every time Rissa looked up, it seemed as though the woman was hanging on Antonio's every word. At one point Donna had even been hanging on to him physically.

Enrico Mazzini suddenly materialised at her side. He was

the last person Rissa wanted to see, but she pinned on a pleasant smile.

'I have just completed a tour of your house, Contessa. You are to be congratulated, both on your vision for the *palazzo* and your catering.'

Antonio was closing in on them. Every time he'd sought her out with his eyes today some other man had seemed to be claiming her, and this time it was his worst enemy. Yet again, he thought, Mazzini has her cornered.

'The Contessa and I have urgent business to discuss, Signor Mazzini.' Antonio's fingers closed around Rissa's elbow and he steered her deftly into a position where any man wishing to speak to her would have to get past him first.

Mazzini did not look happy. He looked even less delighted when Donna sashayed up to take possession of his arm.

Rissa smiled up at Antonio, trying to soften his expression. 'Today has been a great success, hasn't it?'

No—success for me would have been ravishing you in your newly completed suite, he thought. But what he said was, 'Isn't it time you brought things to a close, Larissa?'

It was exactly what Rissa had been thinking.

'How? I can't very well start clearing the tables. It would seem so…obvious.'

'Just stand on the front steps and say a few words.'

Rissa hesitated. Antonio was standing so close to her that she was enveloped by his shadow. She could feel the electric thrill that seemed to crackle from his dark eyes. If she dismissed everyone then he might go too, and that was not what she wanted.

'What is stopping you, Larissa? Is there something wrong? You cannot have disapproved of me rescuing you from Mazzini.'

Rissa was silent for a moment, looking down at her hands as she tried to form an answer.

'No…it's quite the reverse, Antonio. The truth is… Look, I haven't been able to get you out of my mind since the night we met, and…' Her voice died away. She gazed up at him expectantly.

It was the moment Antonio had been waiting for. 'Then go up there and get rid of all these people!' he growled, his voice low with intent.

Ducking past him, Rissa ran up the front steps of the *palazzo* and turned to face her remaining guests. She was on fire, and hoped everyone would think it was nothing more than nerves. She clapped her hands to get their attention.

'Thank you all for coming,' she announced, scanning the crowd. Although she was careful not to look in Antonio's direction, she could feel his eyes boring into her. 'I hope you have all enjoyed yourselves…'

Rissa's mind was racing as she said nice things about the builders' work and Livia's cooking, and then wished them all a good evening. A round of applause greeted the end of her speech—and one immovable Antonio, planted squarely between Rissa and her escape route into the house.

'You dark horse,' he murmured, his lips lifting into a grin. 'If only they knew why you were so keen to dismiss them.'

Rissa gathered all her courage and looked directly into his deep, delicious eyes. It had to be said. 'Before… anything happens, Antonio, there's something you should know about me.'

She paused. Behind them the guests were disappearing, like her conviction, into the dusk. Bats began to flicker around the twilit garden.

Over the years women had flattered Antonio into bed, deceived him into it, and used every other trick in the book. Now the great Contessa Larissa Alfere was trying to join in the game.

'No!' Antonio pulled himself up to his full, imposing height. 'I will accept no more excuses, no more words. It is time for me to take you,' he murmured.

In the distance they heard Livia call out a goodbye as she closed the estate gates behind the last guests. When the house-keeper went inside, they were left completely alone together in the garden. His lips parted in a smile of triumph, but Rissa needed to speak.

'The problem is that, despite Luigi, I'm still a virgin, Antonio.' She went on quickly, before he could laugh, 'I don't know if I can live up to your expectations. That first night— when I fell down the bank and you rescued me—you awakened my body in a way that my husband had never managed, not in five years of marriage. Since that moment I have ached for you, craved you. That is the truth...' Her words struggled out individually, each one waiting for his scorn.

Antonio watched her carefully. He was shocked by her revelation. It would have been the easiest thing in the world to say yes, but the fear in her eyes made him wary. He wanted to be sure she was ready.

Rissa was taut with anticipation. She had wanted to remain cool and impersonal. Instead she felt hot and flustered. She should have put things differently, but it was not the easiest thing in the world to say. Surely if Antonio had really been receptive to her he would not have held back for so long? Perhaps he had only been toying with her instincts? Perhaps he was keeping all his love for Donna...?

'And now you want to give yourself to me?' he said sternly.

Rissa felt herself redden with shame. 'Yes,' she nodded, head down. 'I *want* you, Antonio. And I need—' She stopped.

'What?'

'I need a child to carry on the Alfere name. Everyone says so—Livia, her friends—'

He cut her short with an explosion of disgust. 'You think I would be a pawn in a game like that? For goodness' sake, Larissa, you should adopt a child, if you feel so strongly.'

'No. Perhaps it was a stupid idea after all.' Rissa could hardly speak for regret. Now she was embarrassed. This wasn't going quite as she had wished.

'I don't see why not, if you are so keen to raise another little Alfere. The gossip columns will have a field-day if you take in a photogenic orphan. You could cement your position as Saint Larissa, the grieving widow.'

The mocking tone of his voice lit her reaction. 'I'm not interested in photo opportunities, Antonio. I need a child of my own. A child that only you can give me, because it is only you that I truly want!'

'In his soundbites, Luigi Alfere was always angling for pity because you were infertile,' Antonio retorted, remembering his research.

He had gone too far. 'That was never true.' Her eyes blazed with pain. 'It was the official line, put out for public consumption. I felt so sorry for him, I agreed to the story. My only fault was incompatibility. Somehow it never seemed to work between us. I always loved Luigi, but it was never enough,' she finished sadly.

'I see,' Antonio said slowly. 'But why me? How do you know I would make a fit father? You cannot simply sleep with anyone these days,' he mocked.

Rissa was out of her depth. 'You aren't anyone, Antonio. I have learned enough about you since you have been working here to know that you would be far too sensible to put your own health at risk. The care you take over your work has convinced me of that.'

He laughed, a rich, full-throated sound that made the crickets chuckle on the dusky bank below the terrace where they stood.

'How right you are, Contessa. I always take the greatest care of everything,' he murmured. 'And now, the time for talking is over.'

CHAPTER NINE

His voice had been low with anticipation. A tremor flashed through Rissa's body, its turbulence focussed on the depths of her being. She could say nothing, but as Antonio pulled her into his arms a gasp escaped from her lips.

His hands roamed over her back, then his fingers dug into the smooth pleat of her hair and brought her face close to his. Without waiting for her to reply he kissed her, hard, until her head swam and she gripped ineffectually at his powerful shoulders.

'Antonio! Not here—what are you doing?'

'Isn't it obvious?' His eyes were flashing dangerously with lust. Kissing her again, he probed the soft willingness of her mouth with his tongue. Finding no resistance, his left hand moved to her shoulder, caressing its way around to cup her breast.

Rissa felt her body melt into warm syrup as Antonio's fingers worked their way beneath her top. He had the hands of an artisan, firm and assured. As they ran over her lacy, insubstantial bra she felt the fabric catch and dissolve, but she did not care. Pulling the restraining cups away, he freed the full magnificence of her breasts. For a second his kisses paused as he found the peak of her nipple with his thumb and fingertip, teasing it into wakefulness. Before her eyes closed, Rissa saw his face transported with desire, his lips slightly parted. Seconds later she felt his teeth grazing her neck, nipping at her earlobes in an orgy of sensuality. Tremors of excitement took a direct line from his kisses through her body.

With his right hand, Antonio was massaging her flank, kneading her soft flesh through the thin linen of her skirt, which rode up to give him free access to her bare skin. Rissa was so alight with longing that she became as conscious of his body as she was of her own. As he pulled her closer she felt the large, masculine ridge pushing against the front of his jeans. Instinct took over and she pressed against him, delighting in his sigh of anticipation. Rissa thought of all the occasions when she had wondered what it would be like to go all the way with him, and now here she was, experiencing every heady nuance of Antonio's boundless desire. Greatly daring, she slid one hand down to brush against him.

'Witch,' he growled. 'Go any further and I shall have to take you here in the garden—which I do not intend to do.' Suddenly she was lifted up into his arms. It took almost every grain of his self-control to wait, but he carried her through the echoing house and straight up to her suite. 'Your beautiful new bed is a far more fitting place.'

'Go on, then,' Rissa breathed. 'Take me now, Antonio. Please.'

To have her begging for release like this swept away the last of his restraint. She was torturing him—but two could play at that game, even at this late stage.

'If you are a virgin, how do I know you really mean it?' he taunted her, and was rewarded with a primal cry of desire. He smiled, silently adding that it would be his pleasure. Her clothes were flimsy, and fell aside at his touch. Pushing her back onto the soft insubstantiality of the duvet, Antonio ripped off his own shirt. Kneeling on the bed, he towered over her, bare-chested.

'So—how does my lady like it?'

'I—I don't know…I've never felt like this before,' Rissa heard herself say. It was as though she was living a dream—a fantasy. 'I never experienced anything like this with Luigi…'

Something snapped inside Antonio's head. That name… He never wanted to hear that name again—yet here it was, coming between him and his pleasure. Furious, he flipped Rissa over onto her front and pressed his body down full-length on top of hers.

'You will never speak that name again. Not even in the hottest moments of your passion. I will make you forget him—'

And Mazzini, he thought with a pang. She would have no thoughts of other men in her head when Antonio made love to her. He wanted to fill Rissa entirely—her senses, her mind and above all her body. She would be so full of him that there would be no room left for anyone or anything else. His powering need for her was engulfing him like a tidal wave and would not be denied.

He had to be the one who drove all others from her life. The rogue male within him was about to take exclusive possession of his woman. He paused minutely. What was that about *his* woman, all of a sudden? He'd had so many over the years. He had got the measure of them long ago. And yet…

'Forget who?' Rissa breathed huskily, her mind a heady mix of sensations. She reached back to touch the smooth plane of his muscular arm. It was the moment when she realised with a rush that she had a desperate need to gain fulfilment from his body. It was a want she had never experienced so violently before, and she tried to stifle the thought.

Antonio was looking at her curiously. The fire in her eyes as she looked back at him was a nice touch, accentuating the tigerish longing in her voice. She was an accomplished liar, if nothing else.

'So, you are ready to give yourself to me in order to continue the Alfere line?' His harsh words made her gasp.

'We aren't talking about that now,' Rissa pleaded. 'We're talking about wanting and needing. You want me. I need you.'

'The hired help?' Antonio queried.

'You know what you are worth, Antonio,' Rissa murmured.

He growled into her neck, burying his face in the fragrant flow of her hair.

She came alive at his touch. As he leaned over, pressing his chest against her spine and nuzzling the nape of her neck, all thoughts flew away. Only feelings were left. As their bodies moved together she became more and more receptive to his touch, until every centimetre of her skin was glowing. Twisting beneath him she ran her fingers through his hair, pulling his head down to nuzzle again at the sensitive peaks of her nipples. This time there could be no going back. When she cried out now it was in anticipation. Her senses were running wild.

As Antonio covered her breasts in kisses, the shadows criss-crossing the bedroom grew darker and the breeze from the garden running over her body was more deliciously perfumed than ever. Her bedlinen had never felt so crisp or cool. It was so quiet that she could hear Antonio's breathing change as he drank in the warm fragrance of her. Feeling the warm pressure of his erection against her thigh, Rissa moved to appreciate his body as much as he was enjoying hers.

'No.' He caught her hand before she could make intimate contact with him. 'Don't do that. I like to stay in control—as I am sure you already know.'

He slipped away from her then, but without losing body contact. Rissa was delirious with need. Muscles low down in her stomach were cramping with it. He felt the tightening and met pressure with pressure, sliding a finger between the delicate folds of her femininity and using tiny movements to coax the honey of her arousal. It was too much for Rissa. Arching her body, she opened like a flower, calling desperately for his love.

The moment had come. He responded by riding into her with smooth, easy thrusts. They surfed together through waves of mounting passion, engulfed in kisses and caresses that made them rulers of their own paradise.

Next morning, Antonio tried to counter pleasure with pain as he jogged along the still-dark road. How many women had he taken in the past? He tried to bring some cold common sense to the subject. For some reason his mind refused to compute. The hard fact was that none of those other conquests mattered any more. Rissa was different. She had been as stiff as a cypress. Now she was as sweet and warm as honey. She had changed.

It's not my problem, he told himself briskly. That attitude had levered him out of her arms before she woke, and sent him off on this five-kilometre run before sun-up. He put his head down and sprinted hard for another few hundred metres. The going was tough. It was all uphill, and by the time he reached the next crest his breath was coming in ragged gasps. Pausing, he regrouped his thoughts.

Work on the Palazzo Tiziano was complete. She would expect that to be the end of the matter—job done, so *ciao*, Antonio. That might be her arrangement—but it was not his. She had the house, but he still wanted it. This was not supposed be happening. He had intended to marry Rissa, get the house, then dispense with her. Now she had the house, and was going all-out to secure a family line of her own. Antonio knew it was time to act before *he* became the dispensable one…

This was a good vantage point for looking back down the valley. As he watched, a sliver of sun rose above the distant hillside. He could just make out the *palazzo*'s roof, shining in the first beams of dawn. Down there, the ancient woodwork would begin to click and creak as it expanded in the growing warmth. Fabio would be mewing to be let out of the back door. Coffee and *biscotti* would be perfuming the air as Livia started work. And Rissa would be waking soon, roused by the chirrup of sparrows prancing along all those ridged red tiles.

Taking a deep breath, Antonio started to jog back down the hill.

He had planned to take a quick shower in the ground floor wet room before surprising Rissa with breakfast in bed. Instead, she surprised him. He was still busy soaping down when the bathroom door opened and she walked in.

'Antonio?' Her voice was husky with desire.

He sighed. It was exactly as he had predicted. Virgins were like seal pups—lay a finger on either, and they would follow you everywhere. He remained aloof, but there was no hiding his physical response as she opened the shower door and stepped inside. Head down, meek as a geisha, she knelt in the water that had coursed down his body and kissed him. The thought of her small pink tongue tantalising him towards still more delights made him moan with pleasure. Leaning back against the tiled wall, he enjoyed the contrasting sensations of the cool needles of water and her warm, soft mouth. Adjusting the thermostat, he drew her up and pulled her into his arms. The shower was soaking them both, droplets beading his chest and her hair.

Filling his palm with citrus shower gel, he enrobed her head with bubbles, soaping her body until it glittered. Rivulets ran over her breasts and belly. He scooped them up and used the silken softness to slide his hands over her thighs and bottom. The dark triangle of curls hiding her femininity foamed beneath his fingers, and with a sob of excitement she pressed against his palm as he sought out her path of pleasure. He found that watching her abandonment and knowing that he could make it even better for her gave him almost as much of a kick as the anticipation of his own orgasm.

'You are a wicked, wanton girl,' he murmured into her hair. 'I have never known a woman so willing.'

She looked up at him, still hazy with desire, but with one part of her mind unable to believe what she had just heard.

'What did you say?'

He grinned. 'If I wasn't the seasoned lover that I am, you would wear me out. No lesser man could cope with your demands.'

'Do you mean that?'

'One so beautiful and arousing should not be let out of bed without a bodyguard. That is how serious I am.'

With a mew of delight she fell into his arms again. He responded by lifting her off her feet, taking her weight as she twined her legs around his waist and accepted his love again.

No, not love—*lust*, she tried to tell herself afterwards, when they had reached her bed again in a tangle of towels. This man was acting on nothing more than instinct. That was the arrangement.

Turning her head into the soft white pillow, she squeezed her eyes shut and tried not to cry.

CHAPTER TEN

RISSA woke alone the next day. She had learned that Antonio was a light sleeper, and wondered if that was her influence. When he brought coffee and rolls for her breakfast, she had another reason to worry. His face was troubled, and he seemed distracted. The dream is over, she thought. Now the nightmare begins.

'Is there anything wrong, Antonio?'

'No. No, of course not,' he said abruptly. 'I need some fresh air, that is all.'

Rissa tried to keep her voice light. If he needed to escape, the last thing she wanted was to keep him trapped. 'Why don't you take your pride and joy out for a spin?'

'Why not? How soon can you be ready? I will fetch the Ferrari.'

'You want me to come too?'

His expression was enigmatic. 'Yes.'

They had to stop for petrol high above Monte Piccolo. Rissa got out of the car to stretch her legs. The breeze that always played through the hills lifted her thin cotton skirt as she studied the newspaper headlines on a display rack. Innocently, she was arousing the interest of several men drinking coffee in the shade of an ancient walnut tree. When she strolled over to lean against the stone wall separating the country road from a tumbling slope below, Antonio's eyes never left her.

'Come on. Let's get home.'

Rissa regarded him warily as he pulled out of the petrol station. It was odd that he seemed to think of the *palazzo* as his home, but then, she reasoned, he had been living and breathing the place for months.

Antonio was the last member of the building team left on site. Peace had descended after weeks of destruction, but it had been replaced for her by a secret sadness. Soon Antonio, like her first Italian summer and its swallows, would be gone.

'I am having second thoughts about our arrangement.'

Here it came. He was going to announce the end of their affair. Rissa dug her fingernails into her palms. She hid her hands in her lap so that he would not see. Following his past examples, she kept quiet, persuading him to speak by her silence.

'Our couplings should stop, Contessa.'

Still she said nothing. Antonio changed hands on the steering wheel. Staring at the road ahead, he whipped the Ferrari through a switchback of hairpin bends. Out of the corner of his eye he saw Rissa blanch and screw her fists into tiny balls, but still she did not fling herself on his mercy. Taking her to the edge of fear had not released her feelings into words.

'The only way you can begin the new Alfere dynasty is to find someone to love.'

'I thought I loved Luigi, but it never happened then.' *The difference is that I know I love you,* Rissa cried out silently to herself. *But that's the last thing you want to hear from a woman.*

'It will—one day.' Antonio tried to catch her eye, but her

head was bent. 'Come, Larissa—I have something for us back at the house. I have been saving it for just such an occasion.'

When she did not reply, he put his foot to the floor and drove.

Antonio's Ferrari was abandoned to cool down below the front terrace. He disappeared towards the kitchen while Rissa wandered slowly in through the *palazzo*'s great front doors.

'Vintage champagne, but only ordinary glasses from which to drink it,' he announced, when he had sought her out again. Removing the cork, he poured her a foaming measure.

'You drive a magnificent car, and now you present me with this? Your firm must think highly of you to pay you so well.'

'I am a perfectionist,' he said simply.

'Why don't we take a walk around the house now, and admire your handiwork?' Rissa suggested. 'It is Livia's day off, so we won't be disturbed.'

They went from room to room in near silence. Rissa was delighted with her completed home, but Antonio kept finding something to do. There were always window frames to be inspected or handles to be rubbed over with a cuff.

'It's as though you love this place as much as I do, Antonio.'

He gave a humourless laugh, his dark eyes guarded. 'It pleases me.'

'Then don't leave straight away,' she said impetuously. 'Stay a while longer.'

He did not answer, but took the bottle and refilled her glass. She accepted it with a smile and they continued their leisurely tour of the *palazzo*. It took a long time and the rest of the champagne to reach the ground floor again.

'And to think—this is my home.' Rissa gazed around the main salon in wonder.

Antonio knew his mind should have snapped *No, it's* my *home*. But for some reason—the champagne, the Indian summer, or the end of the project—it didn't. Instead, he took her glass and placed it on the table.

'Yes, but it is *my* creation, Contessa. A combined effort that should be celebrated.'

Her lips parted, and the telepathy developing between them meant that Antonio did not need to ask. They fell into each other's arms again, ready to feed the flames of their desire once more. Without waiting to strip off, Antonio lifted her onto the table. Rissa locked her ankles around his neck and, pushing their clothing aside he took her hard and fast, right there beneath the largest equestrian portrait.

'A fitting tribute, I think,' Antonio said breathlessly as he helped her down.

Rissa could not answer. Her feet might be on solid ground once more, but her body was still in orbit.

The furniture restorer who called later that morning was a typically handsome Italian in his forties. He had brought his young apprentice along, to get some public relations experience, but the lad was having difficulty concentrating. He was standing in the grandest country house he had ever seen, and being spoken to by a *contessa*—one who had great legs, too.

'Quite a few good pieces were lying around the house when I moved in,' Rissa was saying, but the restorer shook his head and looked doubtful.

'I am sorry to tell you that there is nothing of any great value among them, Contessa. You will wish to fill your house with period-correct antiques, of course—?'

'Good grief, no!' Rissa could hear euro signs clocking up at an alarming rate, then realised she might frighten the two men if she started pleading poverty. 'I won't be doing that to begin with, anyway. There is no point in replacing perfectly good furniture. It may have been in storage for some time, but once everything has been cleaned and re-upholstered it will be fine.' They were standing in the room Rissa hoped would one day become a library. Right now she could not justify buying a daily newspaper, let alone paying out money for books. For now, the large salon was filled only with sunlight and echoes.

'It is all in different styles,' the apprentice argued, when he could tear his gaze away from the inviting curve of Rissa's breasts.

'I've thought of that. If you could re-upholster it all in the same design and fabric, that would give the whole job lot unity. It isn't as though the furniture will be close enough to be compared. This big old barn of a place needs seats far and wide, scattered all over the place.'

The door opened and Antonio strode in. Rissa began to smile, but stopped as soon as she saw the look of determination on his face.

'Gentlemen, this is Antonio Isola, my—'

'I have come to collect you, Contessa. We have business to discuss—over a working lunch, I think. So if you would excuse us, gentlemen?'

Rissa smiled and clapped her hands together to draw her meeting to a close. 'Well! That sounds like an offer I can't refuse.'

'Why do you say that?' Antonio looked at her sharply. She had misjudged his mood again, and regretted it.

'It's just a saying. Now, gentlemen, I think we have finished here, so I will say goodbye and look forward to seeing some fabric samples in due course.' Rissa had to throw the last few words over her shoulder as Antonio hustled her out of the room.

'That wasn't very polite, Antonio!'

'It was not very polite of *them* to undress you with their eyes like that. It is good that I arrived to take you away from them.'

They never got as far as going out for lunch. Antonio put his proposition in terms more eloquent than any words. Their picnic tray lay abandoned, along with the trail of clothes they'd left scattered from the door of Rissa's room to the huge luxury of her bed.

Antonio was content to lie and watch her doze. Warm afternoon sunlight filtered through the curtains, which moved in a sigh of breeze from the fragrant garden. Rissa stirred, then paused. Thinking he was still asleep, she eased her way out from under his protective arm and went over to look out of the window. He was happy to admire the sleek line of her naked body from a distance, until she raised one hand and rubbed the back of her neck. In an instant he moved from the bed to her side.

'What is the matter, Larissa? Do you have a headache?'

She nodded.

'It must be lack of food. You should have your lunch—but first…' He replaced her hand with his own, running his thumbs from nape to hairline. The muscles there were taut with tension.

He worked to ease them as she gazed out across the private garden she had made below her room. That had been the place where Antonio had first touched her with intent. She had wasted a lot of time since then, but she was determined to make up for that now.

'Antonio…' she said at last. 'Despite all those brave things I said about carving a future here for myself, I…I'm beginning to feel that my emotions might be getting the better of me.'

For a second his fingers stopped their circling. Then he resumed the long slow strokes of his massage, trying to ease the tension that was growing in her neck despite his efforts. 'Are you trying to tell me something, Larissa?'

'It won't be something you want to hear.'

'Try me. I have heard it all in the past, believe me.'

'I know. That is why it is so difficult for me to open my heart to you now.'

He chuckled. 'You are talking about hearts? That is a bold move when speaking to one of your workforce.'

'That's the problem. You're the last one left at the *palazzo*, and I've come to depend on you. What happens when you've gone, and the next disaster comes around the corner? The truth is I don't have any money, Antonio.'

There. She had said it. If he was only after her money, that would surely put an end to everything. He said nothing. Gathering up her remaining courage, Rissa carried on. 'This place is going to have to be mortgaged to the hilt to settle the remaining costs. That's my only chance of getting any money until the Tiziano estate starts bringing in cash.'

'Money isn't everything.'

She heard the smile in his voice, but before she could reply he bent his head close to her ear and kissed the lobe with infinite gentleness.

Rissa turned to him in wonder. At that moment she thought their minds fused, working as one. It was the ultimate high—loving him with a clear conscience and no secrets between them.

He kissed her again, and again.

'If it wasn't for all my cash-flow problems I would ask you to stay here longer, but to expect you to live in poverty wouldn't be fair.' Rissa sighed. 'Oh, how I wish money could make itself.'

'Let it.' Antonio nuzzled across her cheek and began nibbling her ear. 'The best things in life, like making love, are free.'

Rissa was tempted, but her money troubles were like an elephant in the corner of the room. No matter how much she desired Antonio, the moment was lost. He could feel it, too.

'What is the matter, Larissa?'

'Nothing.'

'You are more tense now than when I began your massage,' he murmured. 'Don't tell me that money is going to come between us?'

'No—no, it isn't that, Antonio.' She slipped her fingers between his and squeezed his hand. 'The trouble is that I've got myself cornered into another awkward situation with Signor Mazzini, and I can't see a way out.'

It was Antonio's turn to stiffen. 'Is he still bothering you?'

'No! Not in the way you might think.'

'Then you are having trouble with his accounting?'

There was no point in denying it. Antonio was too clever.

'I think I may have been giving him too much freedom over the arrangements for this place. He's always resented your suppliers undercutting his contacts. A few weeks ago I refused to pay a bill for consignments you had not ordered. He merely settled the account on my behalf, and added the cost to the quarterly administration bill he sent me this week.'

'Have you ever signed anything to state that he could act in that way?'

'No—Luigi's solicitor in New York appointed him as my agent. *I* haven't signed anything.'

'This is outrageous. Have you made him promise that it will not happen again?'

'Yes. I have written to him saying that if he acts in that way a second time I shall find another agent, and I sent a copy of my letter to the solicitor in Manhattan.'

'But on this occasion you have settled his bill?'

Rissa nodded, and gulped at the memory of it. 'It has just about cleaned me out again. I don't even know if I can survive financially until the mortgage goes through on this place. It is that close. I am so worried. Every letter from the bank sends me further down the road to ruin.'

'That is what Mazzini is counting on. He has always been keen to get his feet under the table here. Don't worry, Larissa. There can be no more trouble with the bank. Now that the work here is finished, getting a mortgage to repay the last few bills and give you some working capital will be a formality. There are only cosmetic touches needed.'

A shudder ran through her body. Antonio's movements became more caressing.

'Do not worry, Larissa. We will manage.'

He bent and kissed her hair. Rissa closed her eyes, hardly able to believe what she was experiencing. Antonio had said 'we'. For the first time in years it felt as though she could relax in security. At last someone was in her corner. She would not have to fight alone. As he took her in his arms she flowed around him.

Antonio felt her body mould to his as he swept strokes over

the smooth flare of her naked hips. The supple joy of her created its own reaction in him. He felt the pressure coiling his stomach muscles as his hands found their own way up to her breasts, cupping gently. She responded by turning to him and accepting a long, lingering kiss. Lifting her into his arms, he carried her back to the bed. It was still tumbled from their last lovemaking. In that warm, soft haven he coaxed Rissa into whispering her desire. As she trembled in anticipation, his hand drifted over the delicate curls of her mound. Her legs parted in anticipation and she moaned, eager for his touch. His finger found the little bud of her clitoris and circled it, bringing her almost to the peak of excitement. She reached for him, delicately stroking his insistent maleness.

'Sometimes only a kiss will do,' he murmured huskily, moving out of reach of her fingertips. Rissa's sigh of disappointment morphed into a moan of pleasure as he spread the swollen lips of her sex gently, and kissed the rose-pink heart of her femininity. A million sparkles ran through her veins. In her innocence she had never dreamed anything could make her feel so wanton and wanted. She arched her body, desperate for him to drink in her pleasure. He moaned with growing desire, and the sound brought her to a new peak of excitement. As his tongue teased her, he reached up to dance his fingertips over her nipples, igniting a thousand more darts of tingling fire. As she reached the summit of delight he entered her.

Her body accepted him, the core of her being rippling with a pleasure that he echoed with low moans of fulfilment.

'Oh, why did it take me so long to surrender to you?' she breathed, encircled by Antonio's protective arms. 'You have made me the happiest woman in the world, Antonio. I am so very, very lucky.'

CHAPTER ELEVEN

WHEN Rissa woke next day she stretched out for Antonio, but he was not there. Glancing at the clock, she smiled. It was nearly eight o'clock. He would already be hard at work on his computer in the site office. Perhaps he might be persuaded to take coffee with her, among the flowers that were making such a pretty picture in her newly restored garden? It would distract him from lining up his next building job, too.

Despite everything, Antonio still kept an eye on his business. Rissa had a terrible fear that when he found something suitable he would be off again. He had already spoken in general terms about his office, although it had been in passing. Rissa had not bothered to question him about his usual work. That was not important. Only Antonio's presence in her home mattered to her. Anything that kept him here for a little while longer was worth trying.

She cleaned her teeth and showered, smiling again at the faint mark on her calf. Antonio's teeth had grazed her skin when she had driven him beyond endurance again during the night. She thought of how her lonely, unfulfilled marriage to Luigi had been put behind her. Antonio certainly had no complaints!

Already wondering happily what they would do today, she

felt her dreamy expression change as she caught sight of something. There was a sheaf of papers on the *chaise longue*. Antonio must have left them behind by accident. It was easy enough to do—when the door of the *en-suite* bathroom was open, it hid that corner of the room. Dressing quickly, she went over and picked them up. Antonio might need them. Love danced in her eyes at the knowledge that he would have been too considerate to come back and disturb her after the turbulent night they had enjoyed. Then she saw the engraved heading on each sheet of heavy, top-quality writing paper. The words *AMI Holdings* were burned in black across every white page.

That could mean only one thing. Antonio was a traitor. He was corresponding with the firm that had wanted to buy the Tiziano estate. The realisation swept away Rissa's scruples and she began to read. The first few letters made no sense. They referred to charitable donations, to properties and places outside of Italy. None mentioned the Palazzo Tiziano—and then she reached one typed letter about a bill for the suite at the Excelsior she had visited with Antonio. AMI Holdings had settled it in full. At the bottom of the letter Antonio's distinctive handwriting noted that the amount had been reimbursed from his private account. All the details were there: dates, times and, most damning of all, the full signature of Antonio Michaeli-Isola.

The man who had stolen her heart was in reality the driving force behind AMI Holdings. That company was her enemy. Fear of their grasping ways had made her determined to hang on to the Tiziano estate whatever happened, but she had not expected tactics like this. Antonio had infiltrated every part of her home and her being. It was the ultimate betrayal.

Things began to fall into place. She had thought herself

stupid for letting Mazzini pull the wool over her eyes, but Antonio had blinded her with a much more dangerous weapon—love. Would the man stop at nothing to get her out of her own home, just so that his firm could ruin the place? A horrible thought struck her. She went out to the nearest staircase and ran her hands over the restored newel post and banister. How did she know the work Antonio had supervised was up to standard? What would happen if the building inspectors arrived and told her everything would have to be ripped out again and redone?

She had no money left. Rissa had been relying on the bank mortgaging the *palazzo* within the next few days. She had been spending money she did not really have, but only in the belief that it was an investment in the future of this grand old house. Antonio Michaeli-Isola had known all this, and it made him more dangerous than any Tuscan serpent. At that moment Rissa did not care. She snatched up the papers that had fallen from her fingers, and marched off to confront the snake in his den.

The site office door smashed back with an impressive bang. Rissa stood in the open doorway and thrust the sheaf of papers at Antonio, who was seated behind his desk.

'You lied to me. All you are interested in is getting your hands on my house!'

There was no point in denying it. Antonio stood up. 'At the beginning, yes, I was. But things have changed, Larissa.' His words were confident and laced with authority.

'Stop! I don't want to hear. You played with my emotions. You patronised me at first, because you thought I would soon get fed up with the *palazzo* and you would be able to pick it up for a song. And when that didn't work…' Her voice was dangerously quiet and her dark eyes stung with tears. She let him fill in the rest for himself.

'If your mind has been working so busily, Larissa, then you should also be aware that when my agents made their first move I instructed them to offer far above the market price for the *palazzo*. It was only when you refused to sell that I took matters into my own hands.'

'And when I wouldn't roll over and abandon the place, you put on an act to seduce it out of me.' Her voice dropped to a trembling whisper. 'All those beautiful things you have been saying to me while we…when we… They were all lies!'

'They were never lies, Larissa.' He put out a hand to her, but she shook it off. 'Yes, at first I was completely focussed on the house. That was because I wanted to make sure all the work was finished to my own exacting standards. Then, as time went on—'

'And you discovered I wasn't going to be easy to dislodge, you started making up to me. That was unforgivable, Antonio. You don't want me—you never did. It is only Tiziano that interests you.' She shook her head in disbelief and wiped away her tears. 'Why are you so blinkered? I love this place— but it is only stones and mortar, after all. It is relationships that matter in life, not…*things*. Why can't you see that, Antonio?'

His dark eyes flashed. 'Life is not as simple as you imagine, Rissa. It is more complex.'

It was an echo of the protests she could remember making to him. 'No, it isn't. You have been using me for your own ends, Antonio. You've betrayed my feelings by pretending to care for me when all you wanted was this—my home!' She gestured at the estate outside his window, still with the papers in her hand.

'You are wrong, Rissa. My feelings for you and my need for Tiziano cannot be compared.'

'Don't give me that!' Rissa was in no mood to listen. 'I have been lulled along by the fantasy that you really cared for me, that your words meant something. To think—I was so taken in by you that I told you things about my marriage I have never spoken of before. I confided in you because I thought I could trust you.'

'Rissa!' He slammed his hand down on the table. 'When we became lovers it was in *spite* of what I knew of Luigi and his family, not because I was cast in the same mould—'

'Of course you are!' Rissa cut across his words with a hiss of fury. 'You are so alike it is untrue. I fell for Luigi before I knew he was rich. Once money came into the equation everything was spoiled. Now you have pulled the same trick on me. That hotel suite, the call from Cardiff, the car—I should have known you were not what you seemed. You were hiding your millions and pretending to be an honest worker until you could sweet-talk me out of the little I have left in life.'

'Yes. Yes, I was using you. But that was before I realised my true feelings ran deeper than I thought.' His dark, penetrating gaze almost overwhelmed her.

She stared at him for a long time. Then, gathering all her nerve, she faced him with the question that she knew would mean the end of everything.

'Prove it.'

Antonio was not a man for half-measures. He reached out and dragged her into his arms. Driving his fingers through her hair, he pressed her against his lips, kissing her so hard and for so long that the blood sang in her ears. When he let her go, they were both breathless.

'Marry me, Rissa,' he breathed.

She listened to her beating heart, and then came to an agonising decision. There was nothing left but to put him to a single, vital test. Deep down, Rissa knew there could only be one outcome. She would be left to count down the seconds until the moment when Antonio abandoned her. Tears filled her eyes, threatening to spill out and ruin everything before he had a chance to do it for her. Then, rising on tiptoe, she placed another kiss on his firm, cool lips.

'Yes, Antonio. Yes, I accept…'

Now! Do it now! a voice screamed in her head. Rissa hardened her heart, knowing she had to strike before his widening smile destroyed her nerve for ever.

'Yes, Antonio—let's get married and start all over again. I have already made arrangements to sell the Palazzo Tiziano. Everything was put in motion yesterday. What could be better for us than to make a brand-new beginning together, away from here?'

It happened exactly as she had known it would. His hands were already falling from her. A dark shadow fell across his eyes. A few seconds before, his lips had been soft with warmth. Now they were hardened into a dangerous line.

'Antonio?'

He was drawing away, already heading for the door. It took all Rissa's strength to let him go.

'You have sold my—*our* home. Where do you *think* I am going?'

As Antonio stormed out of the room. Rissa sank to the floor, sobbing as though her heart would break. Everything had happened exactly as she had convinced herself it would. Antonio had only been interested in the Palazzo Tiziano. He had lied to her. He had wanted her house, not her. As soon as the object of his single-minded desire had seemed no longer to be up for grabs, he had dropped her like flawed marble.

Tay Spender was enjoying himself. It was not often that a solicitor—even a Manhattan solicitor—could be certain of getting the better of a billionaire, but today he was acting under a client's instructions. The fact that his client was an extremely beautiful young woman with a still more impressive estate in Italy tipped the balance further in Rissa's favour.

'Let me get this clear in my mind, Mr Michaeli-Isola. You are asking me to ignore my client's express wishes or…you'll do *what*?' he challenged Antonio. 'Are you going to send your boys around, or sneak a horse's head into my bed? I think not.'

'Do not insult me, Mr Spender,' Antonio said in a dangerous voice. 'That is not the way I work. I came here with a perfectly reasonable request—'

'To block a private transaction made by a vulnerable woman merely on your whim? If you believe that to be reasonable, Mr Michaeli-Isola, I suggest you spend a little more time here in the Land of the Free. Sure, money talks in Manhattan, but it has to be a darned sight more polite about it. Good day to you, sir.'

The solicitor bent over the paperwork he had been studying before the tall, impressive intruder had burst into his office.

Antonio had been wound up with anticipation, but as Tay Spender peered at him one last time over his spectacles all the tension left his body. He left the solicitor's office and closed the door firmly behind him. He took the elevator, and walked out of the building with his head high. After all, as Rissa had said, there was more to life than bricks and mortar.

It was then that he realised he could live without the Palazzo Tiziano. It would be a wrench, but if his family had survived eviction then so could he. The only thing he could not live without was Rissa. It had torn him apart to leave her so suddenly, and now he was aching to return. She had not replied to his e-mails, or picked up any of his telephone messages. The sooner he was back in Monte Piccolo, the better. The longing for her was a physical pain inside him. Gradually, he realised, that need for Rissa had replaced all his old gnawing desire for revenge. This was something he had never before experienced in his whole life. This was—

Suddenly it hit Antonio in the solar plexus like a physical blow. He stopped, right there in the middle of the suffocating, streaming sidewalk in the centre of New York City.

This was—*love*.

Rissa stood at a window and watched the last contractor's van drive away from the house. Antonio's image swam in front of her tear-filled eyes. From the moment he'd dashed away she had been desperate to rush after him, to listen to his phone messages and open the mails he had sent, but she had resisted. She could not lay herself open to any more pain from his silver-tongued lies.

He had deceived his way into her heart, and then into her bed. Yet, despite everything, she still loved Antonio so much that it hurt. Only by cutting herself off from him entirely could she hope to heal the wounds that loving him had inflicted on her.

The next time Antonio's distinctive red Ferrari streamed up the drive, Rissa dodged out of sight. She had come to a decision and her bags were already packed. Sales at the market had been bringing in a reasonable amount of money, and she had been saving hard. There was just enough in her account now for a budget flight to England.

It won't be running away, she told herself as she picked up her passport from the new dressing table. I'm overdue a visit, and it won't be long before I'm back here again.

Despite her words, the look she cast around her room had the poignancy of a final farewell. Antonio would take an age to stow his beautiful surrogate child away in its garage. She had a few moments to dream of how things might have been.

When she slipped out of the rear entrance, she took care to remove his set of spare keys to the house from their hiding place beneath a loose cobblestone in the yard. Antonio Michaeli-Isola needn't think that her absence meant he could start lording it over the Tiziano estate. She meant to deny him that pleasure for ever.

She left Monte Piccolo in the same way she had arrived—by taxi. I might be abandoning the place, as the Alfere-Tiziano family did, she thought, but I have to go now, while I still have my pride. One more encounter with Antonio would be sure to rob me of even that, she consoled herself as her driver veered around a bend. Antonio and the Tiziano estate were lost to sight—but not to her heart.

CHAPTER TWELVE

RISSA had lost track. The red-eye connection and the flight passed by in a haze, but she was starting to come to terms with her decision by the time she had worked her way across London. Reaching the Keir Hardy Buildings, she was disappointed that it no longer felt like home. The graffiti and the cars burned out on the windswept wastelands around the tower blocks had not changed, but she had.

It was only when Rissa knocked on the door of Flat 83 that things got back to something like normal. George and Jane Silverdale were thrilled to see her. Within minutes she was being spoiled with a cup of milky tea. It was lovely to be home. She could put all the loneliness behind her.

Luigi had become increasingly distant in the later years of their marriage, leaving Rissa isolated, and the old Contessa, Luigi's mother, had been strong and silent. Between their first meeting and her death, three years later, Laura Alfere had not spoken a single word to Rissa. Luigi's young wife had been ignored in a way that only the truly haughty could manage. The old Contessa had communicated with Rissa only through her servants. This had done little for Rissa's authority and absolutely nothing for her self-esteem. A woman who could behave in the way that Laura Alfere had was capable of anything. Lately Rissa had started to wonder if Antonio's dislike of the family might have been fuelled by more than his simple disdain for the ruling classes.

As soon as she could tactfully extract herself from being fussed over by her parents, she offered to go shopping down in the precinct to pick up a few things. They had insisted she should stay in her old room, rather than find a hotel, and Rissa was glad to do so. All the same, she did not want to impose on them any more than she could help. Despite her offers to pay for the extra shopping, they pressed cash on her, and a list of her favourite British comfort foods.

Rissa had another reason for wanting to escape. She would have to pass the local library to reach the grocer's store. From her earliest days it had been impossible for Rissa to walk by without going in, and today would be no different. On-line information might be able to give her a few more interesting facts about AMI Holdings. Rissa wanted real proof that Antonio was as bad as she imagined him to be. The image of his abandoned love was too painful to bear without an antidote.

Booking an on-line session was easy. By the time Rissa had done all the shopping, and chatted to a couple of old neighbours she had not seen since leaving for university, it was time to check in and settle down in front of the computer. She was absorbed in typing out 'AMI Holdings' in full when a shadow fell across her keyboard. With a smile she looked around, ready to tell the librarian that she was doing fine. Then she froze.

'Antonio!'

'Yes.' Unshaven, and hollow with lack of sleep, he towered

over her like an avenging angel. Rissa tried to stand, but there was no room to push back her chair. He was blocking her escape.

'I left Monte Piccolo without telling anyone where I was going. How did you find me?'

'I have my ways.'

His voice was low and resonant. Rissa tried to gauge his mood, but his face was giving nothing away. The situation must be as intolerable for him as it was for her—after all, she had called his bluff, hadn't she? The fact that he'd had the nerve to track her across Europe when she wanted to lick her wounds in private fired a new anger in Rissa. She narrowed her eyes and squared up to him.

'What you mean is that you have an international network of staff with spies everywhere. First I hear that you hunted down my solicitor, poor Mr Spender, and now you have turned on me.'

He looked down on her steadily. 'Apparently your parents are the only Silverdales in the telephone book.'

Rissa swelled with indignation and slapped her palms down onto the library desk. Half a dozen people looked around at the noise. 'I knew it! You did not even do it yourself. You paid someone to get onto my case,' she hissed in a whisper. 'Although that doesn't explain how you got here from Monte Piccolo so quickly. It took *me* the best part of a day!'

'I flew myself.'

Rissa scowled. 'I know you have money, Mr Isola. That means you can't impress me with the fact now.'

'It is a light aircraft owned by AMI Holdings. It isn't my personal property. What would a man like me do with a thing like that? And my full name is Michaeli-Isola, if you intend to be formal.'

Rissa gasped. 'Michaeli? No wonder your signature looked

familiar. That name appears all around my house.' She stared at him. He stared back.

'That is because the Alfere family took over the ancient estate of Michaeli-Tiziano.'

Everything began to fall into place. Rissa's eyes widened with growing realisation. 'That is why you want my house. That is why you worked for nothing. The Ferrari—that suite in the Excelsior—no wonder you could sell me that story about taking paid leave! The great mastermind behind AMI Holdings probably earns more in his sleep than a hundred ordinary people in a year.'

'Wealth means nothing.'

Rissa looked at the sun-browned, experienced hands that had worked so hard for her house. A tremor ran through her when she remembered that they had been adept at working on her, too. It took an effort to harden her heart to reply.

'You might use it to impress gullible women.'

'True—although I knew better than to try it on you, didn't I?'

They looked at each other for so long that the screensaver cut in on the library computer. Rissa jumped.

'I must finish here and get back home, Mr Michaeli-Isola.'

'What are you doing?'

Rissa knew there was nothing for it but honesty.

'I was trying to find out more about AMI Holdings and their future plans for the Palazzo Tiziano. If they are honest enough to show them on the web, that is.'

'Don't bother about me. It is my family home that is important.' He covered her mouse with his hand and clicked on the data bar. 'Have you tried the name Michaeli?'

'You did not give me a chance to try anything.'

She thought he had taken control of the machine to stop

her. Instead, he typed in the words 'Michaeli-Tiziano', then pushed the mouse back towards her hand. 'It will not make for happy reading.'

'Would you rather I didn't see it?'

'On the contrary—if I had been completely honest with you from the start, Larissa, none of this would have happened. I would have gone to the Italian authorities and had the *palazzo* requisitioned. The case for the restitution of my family is so strong there would have been no argument against me taking possession. I did not have to go to the trouble of offering to buy it from you, but bullying is not in my nature.'

Rissa made a small noise of disbelief. He silenced her with a look. 'Call it a whim, but at first I wanted to take the peaceful, easy way out. If I had gone in with all guns blazing from the start you would have hated me.' He shrugged. 'But that would have meant nothing to me—then.'

His eyes burned with passion now, and it was all for her. Rissa could not resist a gasp. She was held in the power of his gaze and could not turn away.

'How can you be so convinced that my house is yours, anyway?' Rissa's voice sounded faint and faraway. 'Luigi's family were so grand they owned all sorts of property. Any dispute over the ownership of Palazzo Tiziano must date back centuries. No one but the Alfere-Tiziano clan could have any call on it.' Rissa tried to stand up for herself, but her convictions were beginning to waver.

She thought back to Livia's hints. Antonio was totally convinced he was the rightful owner, but Luigi had been so proud of his ancient lineage. Surely there was no way Antonio could have any sort of a valid claim? Anyone in England who harboured a grudge from Civil War days, or who resented their ancestors losing out to William the Conqueror would have to be insane—it was all so long ago. Yet Antonio must be similarly mistaken, and he was the sanest person she had met.

She was watching him. Antonio was watching the screen. Rissa heard him click on a link. Slowly, gradually, she turned to see what was on display.

For long moments she read in silence, then looked at the black and white photograph reproduced on the web page before her. It had been taken on the front steps of her beloved new home. A tall, gaunt woman was clutching the arm of a fat man in a trilby hat and a double-breasted suit. Children in varying sizes surrounded the couple. Standing beside the family group were uniformed men.

Rissa tapped the screen. 'That woman is the image of my mother-in-law! Contessa Laura made the first three years of my marriage a misery. This snap must have been taken a long time ago—during the Second World War, maybe—but there's no doubt about the Alfere family resemblance.' She did not add the 'Tiziano' name this time. As she read the caption, she realised that the wrong done to Antonio's family was recent.

'"Signor Alfere and his wife accept the keys of the Palazzo Tiziano as a reward from a grateful nation,"' she read aloud. 'So that must be Laura's parents—Luigi's grandparents.'

'Your husband's family had mine convicted of helping the partisans, but my grandmother managed to escape and eventually ended up in Naples. She arrived there with nothing more than the clothes she stood up in, and had to make a completely new life for herself. She could never afford to return home, or take her case to the courts. Mind you, our old family curse had the last laugh. Your late mother-in-law was the only child out of that gaggle to survive.' He nodded towards the picture. 'My grandmother always listened out for news from home. The Alferes were so desperate to keep the fine old family name going, they made your husband's father adopt it as his own!'

Rissa was still trying to take it all in. 'And to think I wanted to do everything I could to keep their memory alive.' She shook her head sadly.

'My mother was born in Naples, and never liked to be reminded of what might have been. But I always loved to hear my grandmother's stories about Monte Piccolo. I became determined to regain my family's property. It was always one of those distant dreams that life never gives you the time or opportunity to grab. But when I read reports that the last Alfere was dead, I saw my chance.'

'Why didn't you tell me all this right at the start, Antonio? It hardly seems like a suitable case for "forgive and forget". Your family were evicted from the Palazzo Tiziano, and Luigi's family had no claim to it at all!' Rissa was outraged on behalf of the Michaeli family.

Antonio was holding his small crucifix between finger and thumb, running it up and down its fine silver chain. 'I was not about to speak ill of your husband. He was born long after all this happened, and so was I. Neither of us was in a position to take any moral high ground.'

Rissa was not so sure. 'No wonder Luigi's mother was so horrible to me.'

'Every family has its black sheep.'

'Not yours, I'll bet.'

Antonio almost managed to laugh. 'Do you remember the portrait of that horseman, hanging in the main salon at home?'

Rissa thought back to her dusting—and to their antics on the table below that picture. 'Count Lorenzo, you mean?'

'That's right. He is pointing to his hunting hounds in the distant landscape.'

Rissa frowned, remembering the grisly sight. 'It was hard to make it out under all those dingy layers of soot and varnish, until I climbed a ladder to dust it down. The dogs are tearing a deer to pieces.'

'That's right. Lorenzo is admiring them from horseback.' Antonio nodded.

'But he was so handsome…' Rissa looked at Antonio and scrutinised him carefully. 'Yes…there is quite a family resemblance, now I know that you two are related. I always had the feeling those portraits looked familiar. Thank goodness you don't go in for blood sports, Antonio. You don't, do you?' she added quickly. There was so much she still had to learn about him.

Antonio shook his head. 'In any case, that painting of Lorenzo is an allegory. His first wife had an affair, so he hunted her down with his dogs.'

Rissa recoiled in horror. 'Oh, the poor woman!'

'The Contessa Lucretzia had been an Alfere before her marriage. My grandmother told me all the family stories when I was a child. It was a real pleasure to walk around your house that first time, matching my memories to those portraits. Lucretzia must have been an ancestor of your husband's. If we can find a picture of her, you might be able to spot a family likeness between it and your Laura.' He began another computer search, but Rissa stopped him.

'Don't call her *my* Laura!' She grimaced. 'From this moment on, I don't want her, or Luigi, mentioned ever again.'

Antonio lifted his finger from the mouse button. 'Are you sure?'

Rissa looked down nervously. 'I have never been more convinced of anything in my life.'

Antonio knelt down before her, lifting her chin so her gaze met his.

'Then marry me, and I shall exorcise you totally, right down to the Alfere name.'

Rissa spoke slowly and carefully. 'It is my house you want. You desire the Palazzo Tiziano.'

His fingers gently brushed her cheek. Rissa trembled. *He is going to lie and say no, that's not true, it's me he loves and not the house,* she thought. *He is bound to say no.*

'Yes,' Antonio said, after what felt like an eternity. 'Yes, Larissa, I cannot deny it. From the moment I was old enough to know what great injustices my family had suffered at the hands of the Alferes, I have been determined to reclaim my house. I have always wanted the Palazzo Tiziano more than anything else in this life—until I met you.' His hands slid around her back and pulled her into the longest, most tender kiss she had ever enjoyed.

For a long, luscious time her mind went blank, but as he released her all the darkness flooded back. 'But you couldn't wait to get away from me—you dashed off the moment I told you I had made the decision to sell the estate!'

This was the acid test, but he did not hesitate. 'With hindsight, I can see that was wrong. It was a wrench to leave you then, but I thought I could stop the sale. I had to move fast to try and block any arrangements you had made.'

'You would have gone over my head?' Rissa was aghast.

'I have already said it was wrong. But my reasoning at the time was that we would need somewhere to live once we were married. My idea was that the estate was our perfect home—mine by right and inheritance, and ideal for you because you love the old place. I was unsuccessful in my bid, but it does not matter much.' He grimaced, but managed to add, 'I can live without the Palazzo Tiziano.'

Then his face warmed with a genuine smile of love. 'As long as I can spend the rest of my life with you, I can live anywhere. Although you must promise me one thing, Larissa.'

'Anything,' she breathed.

'I would ask you to delay the sale of your estate in Monte Piccolo until my mother has been able to visit. She has always insisted in living in the present, but I would like her to see the house where her mother and father were so happy, and where she should have been born. I was intending my eventual purchase of the *palazzo* to be a surprise for her,' he finished quickly.

'Antonio! You're *accepting* the fact that I'm going to sell? You would say goodbye to all those centuries of your family's tradition just for me?'

'Of course. Although I must be truthful—it will not be without a pang,' he conceded.

Rissa gazed into his eyes for a long time. If she was going to make a confession, now was the time. But her mind was already working on a grander plan. 'I am so sorry I jumped to the wrong conclusion, Antonio,' she said slowly, giving herself time to think. 'I should have trusted you. Can you ever forgive me for turning my back on you?'

'No apology is needed—only another reply to the question I asked you the last time we were alone together in the Palazzo Tiziano. Will you marry me, Larissa?'

'Oh, Antonio!' she breathed. 'It would make me the happiest woman in the world if I could become your wife—'

A sudden outbreak of applause made them both look round. All the other library visitors had been hanging on their every word.

With all the guile of a natural-born Michaeli-Tiziano, Rissa announced that as she was the official owner of the *palazzo* until midnight on their wedding day, the reception would be held there, on the terrace.

Years of respectable working class life rose up in George and Jane Silverdale—Rissa's adoptive parents. They worried that they would not have anything to wear, would not know how to get there, and finally that they could not speak a word of Italian. Rissa explained that Freddie, her acquaintance the magazine editor, would accompany them from England, and Antonio supplied another lifeline.

'My mother speaks English quite well. She will be able to talk enough for all of you, even when she isn't translating!' he said as they sat in the tiny best room of the Silverdales' flat, drinking tea and eating biscuits.

Jane Silverdale had found a packet of paper doilies somewhere and set the biscuits out on a plate. This made Rissa frown at her mother quizzically, as she was used to eating them straight from the packet. Distracted, Mrs Silverdale noticed her husband dunking a biscuit in his tea. As she opened her mouth to apologise for this slip, Antonio solemnly did exactly the same thing.

'It's the only way to eat them where I come from,' he said innocently to his frantic hostess, as Rissa tried not to laugh.

Antonio and Rissa had told everyone they wanted a small wedding. No one took any notice. The entire population of

Monte Piccolo filled the church. The world's press had to wait around outside. Once the ceremony was over, only invited guests got into the estate grounds—Livia and a scrum of the biggest locals she'd been able to recruit saw to that.

A perfect clear autumn day, with plenty of good local food and drink at the reception, meant the party went on until dark. Livia arranged for lanterns to be set up around the terrace as Rissa slipped away unnoticed. Antonio had disappeared a few moments earlier, after making a secret assignation with his new wife.

She walked slowly up the grand staircase towards their suite. Her fingers danced over the newly restored banister rail, but her mind was troubled. She could see Antonio's silhouette on the upper landing, but there was a dark cloud threatening to stifle their happiness. Reaching the top step, she ran to him through the long gallery, silk and lace whispering as she went.

'Antonio! Listen—there is something I must tell you—'

'You don't need to tell me anything—except how pleased you are to see this again.' He handed her a shallow cardboard box from one of the best dress shops in Florence.

Rissa put it on a side table and lifted the lid. Folded between layers of softest tissue lay the favourite gown she had sacrificed for the *palazzo*. 'My black velvet! Oh, Antonio— you bought it back for me!'

'I knew it would be the perfect present.' He smiled as she held the dress against herself and twirled around.

'It was a shame you didn't give me this straight after we cut the wedding cake—I could have changed into it. Everyone could have seen how generous and thoughtful you are, Antonio.'

'Black is not a colour for weddings,' he said simply. 'And

now I have one last present to unwrap. That is you!' He put the dress aside, his dark eyes flashing an invitation. Lifting her into his arms, he kissed her lightly before carrying her over the threshold of their room.

'No—wait, Antonio. We have to talk.'

'This is not a time for speech. It is a time for presents and—' He laughed, a deep, melodious sound from the depths of his broad chest. 'There is a parcel on our bed! Who is it from?'

'Me, of course. But Antonio, you must listen to me before you open it—'

'But you have already given me my present, Rissa.'

'This is another one. But—'

He reached the bed, but could not put her down, because the large box wrapped in silver paper and trailing ribbons was sitting squarely in the middle of their coverlet.

Antonio set her on her feet, clicking his tongue as he dragged the heavy thing towards him.

'The new laptop was more than enough, Larissa—I didn't expect anything else. I know you are as poor now as you've ever been, and will be until the…' he hesitated '…proceeds of the sale go through.'

'I should hang on to your gratitude until you hear what I have to say. Antonio, listen to me. I had to know for certain if your feelings were for me or this house. The Palazzo Tiziano was never for sale. I lied to you. It was a spur-of-the-moment thing, to see if your proposal was genuine, and now I regret it.'

Antonio's hands slid away from the ancient wooden box he had been unwrapping. He stood up straight. Not for the first time Rissa felt a shiver of apprehension as she saw exactly how big and powerful he was. She began to back away from him.

'That was a risk,' he said slowly. 'When I left you so suddenly, you must have thought your suspicions were right.'

She nodded, her head drooping.

'Then I am sorry, Rissa.'

Her head jerked up. '*You're* sorry? But I was the one who lied—'

'You did that only because you were feeling insecure. Your background with Luigi Alfere had destroyed your self-esteem. I should have realised that, and made my feelings for you unmistakable.' His voice was as soft and caressing as the hand he moved gently over the skin of her cheek.

'Then you accept my apology?'

'None was needed.' His fingers played beneath her chin, lifting it so that he could kiss her. 'Now, are you going to help me unwrap this present, Mrs Michaeli-Isola, so that we can move on to more…intimate treats?' he whispered eventually.

'I hope you did not spend too much on me,' he chuckled as they tore at the paper and ribbons to expose the present.

Rissa slipped her arms mischievously around his waist and hugged him. 'It didn't cost me a thing. Unless you count sleepless nights, scraped skin and broken fingernails, that is!'

Standing behind him, her face pressed against the broad expanse of his back, Rissa could not see what he was doing. His movements became slower, then stopped. She heard the box lid fall from his fingers, and gave him a squeeze.

'Well?'

He did not answer.

'Do you like it?'

'I don't understand.' He turned in her arms. In one hand he held a sheaf of dog-eared, yellowing papers. 'These are deeds to a property.'

'That's right. They are the deeds to *this* property. The Palazzo Tiziano—it's all legally yours.' Rissa smiled up at him. 'The house, the estate—all the bills, all the problems. As they said in the wedding ceremony—for richer, for poorer.'

'But…I thought you said you weren't selling it?' His brow contracted, as it always did when he was trying to puzzle something out. 'So you contacted my people again and arranged to sell it to me? That must be where you got the money for the laptop…'

'No money was involved. It's a present from me to you, Antonio. To keep for ever, with no strings.' She picked up a trail of silver ribbon and let it fall from her fingers, but her smile faded as she realised his expression was not showing the instant delight she had expected. 'I seem to have done the wrong thing, Antonio, and I'm sorry. When you proposed, my reaction was to think you were only after Tiziano. It was an instantaneous thing—I wanted to know for sure that your love for me was real, and not just an excuse to get your hands on your ancestral lands—'

He stopped her words with a kiss.

'Never doubt me,' he said, releasing her from the kiss but not from his arms. 'It was true that when we first met my thoughts were centred on getting my house back. Then I fell in love with you, and suddenly nothing else mattered. I would have seen you give away this *palazzo* without a word. I would have packed my bags and followed you to the ends of the earth. Instead, you have brought me home.'

'It is where we both belong,' Rissa breathed.

Taking her hand, Antonio led her over to the windows opening out onto their newly restored balcony. Down in the garden, celebrations were still going on. Strings of coloured lights threaded through the olive trees blinked in a gentle breeze. From here they could make out the newly planted rose bushes on the edge of the first terrace.

'Just think,' she breathed, 'we are the last of the Michaeli-Tizianos.'

'Ah—there I must correct you, Mrs Michaeli-Tiziano-Isola. I am not the last of my line. I intend to be the first in a new dynasty. Mind you, we may have to consider building a new wing, simply to house all the portraits we will have to get painted.'

Rissa laughed and slipped her arms around him. At that moment, the warm protection of his body was all she needed. 'At least we don't have to worry about any old curse, or the likelihood of earthquakes now that there's a legitimate heir in the house. This *palazzo* should stand for a thousand years.'

MILLS & BOON®

Live the emotion

0107/01b

Modern
romance™

THE ITALIAN BOSS'S SECRETARY MISTRESS
by Cathy Williams
Rose is in love with her gorgeous boss Gabriel Gessi – but her resolve to forget him crumbles when he demands they work closely together…on a Caribbean island! She knows the sexy Italian is the master of persuasion, and it won't be long before he's added her to his agenda…

THE KOUVARIS MARRIAGE by Diana Hamilton
Madeleine is devastated to learn that her gorgeous Greek billionaire husband, Dimitri Kouvaris, only married her to conceive a child! She begs for divorce, but Dimitri is determined to keep Maddie at his side – and in his bed – until she bears the Kouvaris heir…

THE SANTORINI BRIDE by Anne McAllister
Heiress Martha Antonides is stunned when she arrives at her Greek family home – billionaire Theo Savas has taken it over! Forced together, they indulge in a hot affair. But Theo will *never* marry. Although Martha knows she must leave, her heart and body won't obey her mind…

PREGNANT BY THE MILLIONAIRE
by Carole Mortimer
Hebe Johnson has always secretly admired her wealthy boss, but she never believed she'd end up sharing his bed! After one intense and passionate night, Hebe is in love. But Nick doesn't do commitment… And then Hebe discovers she's having his baby…

On sale 2nd February 2007

*Available at WHSmith, Tesco, ASDA,
and all good bookshops*

www.millsandboon.co.uk

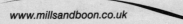

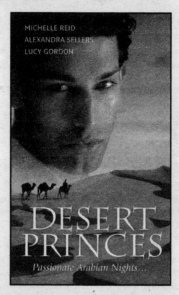

4 FREE

BOOKS AND A SURPRISE GIFT!

We would like to take this opportunity to thank you for reading this Mills & Boon® book by offering you the chance to take FOUR more specially selected titles from the Modern Romance™ series absolutely FREE! We're also making this offer to introduce you to the benefits of the Mills & Boon® Reader Service™—

- ★ **FREE home delivery**
- ★ **FREE gifts and competitions**
- ★ **FREE monthly Newsletter**
- ★ **Exclusive Reader Service offers**
- ★ **Books available before they're in the shops**

Accepting these FREE books and gift places you under no obligation to buy, you may cancel at any time, even after receiving your free shipment. Simply complete your details below and return the entire page to the address below. You don't even need a stamp!

YES! Please send me 4 free Modern Romance books and a surprise gift. I understand that unless you hear from me, I will receive 6 superb new titles every month for just £2.80 each, postage and packing free. I am under no obligation to purchase any books and may cancel my subscription at any time. The free books and gift will be mine to keep in any case.

P7ZED

Ms/Mrs/Miss/Mr ....Initials ....

BLOCK CAPITALS PLEASE

Surname ....

Address ....

....

....Postcode..

Send this whole page to:
UK: FREEPOST CN81, Croydon, CR9 3WZ.